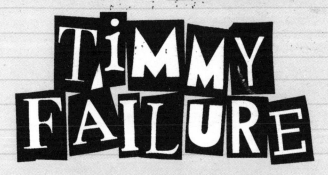

SANITIZED FOR YOUR PROTECTION

Praise for the series

"This inspired book will prompt
outbursts of laughter."
**The Sunday Times 100 Children's
Modern Classics**

"A fabulously fun read ... original
and quirky, with real heart."
Philip Ardagh, *Guardian*

"For Timmy Failure, success
is the only option!"
Lincoln Peirce, creator of *Big Nate*

"Will glue you to the page like
cheese stuck to the carpet."
Adam, aged 9, *Lovereading4kids.co.uk*

"A brilliantly bad detective."
Guardian

"If you are a fan of *Diary of a Wimpy Kid* or
Tom Gates you will be a fan of this series."
Alice, aged 9, *Lovereading4kids.co.uk*

"Seldom has failure been so
likable—or so funny."
The Wall Street Journal

TiMMY FAILURE

SANITIZED FOR YOUR PROTECTION

Stephan Pastis

WALKER
BOOKS

First published in Great Britain 2015 by Walker Books Ltd
87 Vauxhall Walk, London SE11 5HJ

This edition published 2019

2 4 6 8 10 9 7 5 3 1

This book has been typeset in Nimrod

Printed and bound by CPI Group (UK) Ltd, Croydon CR0 4YY

British Library Cataloguing in Publication Data:
a catalogue record for this book is available from the British Library

ISBN 978-1-4063-8721-6

www.walker.co.uk

www.timmyfailure.com

A Shocking Prologue That If All Goes Right Will Make You Want to Read the Rest of This Book

We're all in trouble when we can't tell the good guys from the bad.

But tell that to the photographers that surround the entrance to the hotel.

And tell it to the crowd of onlookers who want a glimpse.

And tell it to the police who try in vain to clear a path.

For the bad guy.

Who at precisely 9:07 p.m. is escorted out of the revolving glass doors of the hotel to an explosion of flashbulbs.

The lingering effect of which produces a bright ball of light in the center of his gaze.

Making it impossible to see the faces of the surging crowd.

As a cop shoves a photographer. And someone screams. And a woman faints.

And the bad guy is pushed through the throng.

His hands now cuffed.

His shoes quite scuffed.

A world gone mad.

The good now bad.

CHAPTER 1

Let the Fireworks Begin

It is a fireworks show like no other.

"Sit back, Timmy," says my mom.

"But I want to watch."

"There's nothing to watch," she says.

And as she says that, another large bug explodes across the windshield of our car.

"Ooooh, that was a big one," I say. "Very colorful, too."

"Timmy, we have hundreds of miles left on this drive," says my mother. "Now sit back or I'm stopping the car."

I sit back. But am hit in the arm by my polar bear.

"Ow!" I yell.

"What now?" asks my mom.

"My polar bear hit me."

It's true. He does it every time he sees a Volkswagen.

"That does it," says my mom, who before I know it is pulling our rental car into the parking lot of an E-Z Daze Motel.

"You can't stop here," I tell my mother. "We're in the middle of nowhere."

But she doesn't answer. She just gets out of the car and says something to Doorman Dave, who has pulled his car in next to ours.

Doorman Dave is my mother's boyfriend. He's called Doorman Dave because he used to be the doorman in our apartment building. But now he got a job far away, so we're using my precious spring break to help him move.

And it is tragic beyond comprehension.

Tragic because I have stared at nothing but cornfields for hundreds of miles.

OH, LOOK...MORE CORN.

Tragic because it has all been to the tune of my mother's favorite country musician, Slim Chitlins.

And tragic because of the effect it is having on a boy a world away.

A boy named Yergi Plimkin.

CHAPTER 2

Meet Yergi Plimkin

Yergi Ismavitch Plimkin is from somewhere that is not here.

And he has no books.

A fact discovered by my peace-loving, world-saving classmate Toody Tululu when she saw Yergi's large face in a newspaper ad.

TOODY TULULU

NEWSPAPER AD

YERGI PLIMKIN'S FAMILY HAS NO BOOKS FOR YERGI TO READ... CAN YOU HELP?

So Toody organized a charity, Yergi Ismavitch Plimkin, You Are Poor. While the name wasn't flattering, the acronym was catchy:

And so YIP YAP held bake sales and car washes and bike races until it had raised enough money to buy poor Yergi Plimkin some books.

That amount being:

"Zero dollars and twelve cents," read YIP YAP's vice president, Nunzio Benedici.

"What?" exclaimed a shocked Toody Tululu at the monthly meeting of YIP YAP. "Read that again, Madam Vice President."

"I'm a boy," replied Nunzio. "I can't be a Madam."

"Read it again, anyway."

So Nunzio read the amount again.

"That can't be," said Toody Tululu. "We had one hundred and twenty dollars at our last meeting and we haven't spent a dime."

"I don't know what to tell you," said Nunzio, looking at the ledger. "It's not there."

And with that, peace-loving Toody made a brief, yet cogent, statement.

SOMEONE WILL DIE FOR THIS!!!!!

CHAPTER 3

Let's Do the Timmy Warp Again

```
When all your money's
Been seized by a criminal,
Call Timmy Failure
And not Timmy Fiminal.
        —Timmy Failure jingle[1]
```

To the best of my knowledge, everyone on earth has now read the prior three volumes about my life.

---

1. Yes, I am aware that there is no one named Timmy Fiminal. But there is no other word that rhymes with *criminal*. And besides, I'm a detective, not a poet.

If, however, you have spent the last few years living under a rock:

Or at the bottom of the sea:

Or in a time warp:

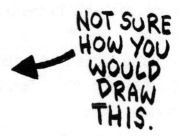

NOT SURE
HOW YOU
WOULD
DRAW
THIS.

Then let me fill you in.
My name is Failure. Timmy Failure.

ME

DISTINCTIVE
SCARF

I am the founder, president, and CEO of Failure, Inc., the greatest detective agency in town, probably in the country, perhaps in the world.

The name of the agency used to be *Total* Failure, Inc. The "Total" being my business partner, Total.

← BUSINESS PARTNER, TOTAL

But then I fired him.

And now he lies in bed eating bonbons.

The degree to which that bear has abused our professional relationship is both astonishing and embarrassing.

And will not be discussed here.

And besides, I want to get back to the story.

So let me sum up everything you need to know as concisely as possible so we can get on with things:

     1. Me Timmy.

     2. Timmy great.

     3. Bear fat.

And with that understood, you now know why it was that when YIP YAP got tip-tapped,[2] they called the one man who could help them.

And it wasn't Timmy Fiminal.

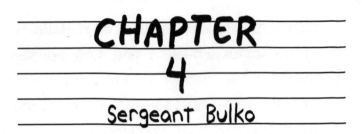

CHAPTER 4

Sergeant Bulko

"Start at the beginning," I tell my best friend, Rollo Tookus.

Rollo Tookus

Stanfurd

"YIP YAP's money is gone," says Rollo.

"I know *that*, Rollo. I mean, why are you involved?"

"I'm the sergeant-at-arms. They said it was my job to find out what happened."

"What's a sergeant-at-arms?"

"I don't know."

"Did you join the military?"

"I don't think so."

"Are you armed?"

"No."

"So what is it?" I ask.

"I don't know," answers Rollo. "All I know is that it was the only elected office that YIP YAP didn't have filled. And holding an elected office looks good on a college application. As does participation in band, speech tournaments, civic organizations—"

His head begins to shake.

It is something that happens whenever the topic of grades, college, or his future arises.

So I do what only a friend can do.

I hit him with a tetherball.

"What'd you do that for?" asks Rollo.

"You were going to your unhappy place. I was saving you."

He tosses the tetherball back at me. It strikes me in the cranium.

"Oh, God," I exclaim as I fall to the pavement. "I've been concussed. Someone call the authorities."

But Rollo does not call the authorities.

So we do what only good friends can do:

We spend the next five minutes hitting each other with the tetherball.

"Well, that was productive," I tell him.

"You started it," Rollo answers.

"Yeah, well, you needed it."

"And you assaulted a member of the military," Rollo replies, checking his corduroy trousers to see if he has split them open.

He gets up and walks off.

"I haven't finished asking you questions," I call out to him.

"Do it later," he shouts back over his shoulder. "Some of us have to get ready for the history test."

"What history test?" I ask.

CHAPTER
5

Don't Know Much About History,
But Know a Lot About Mysteries

Name: TIMMY FAILURE

Great Explorers
History Exam

1) Who was Meriwether Lewis?

I don't know, but I find it hard
to believe that any parent could
name their child Meriwether.

2) Who was William Clark?

Probably someone who made fun
of Meriwether.

3) Why did Meriwether head west?

To get away from William.

"I think I aced that," I whisper to Rollo.

"Quiet," replies Rollo. "I'm not finished."

"Tell me more about YIP YAP. Like who else is in the group."

"Hush," says Rollo.

"I need to know," I tell him. "Everyone's a suspect until proven otherwise."

I feel a hand on my shoulder.

"There's no talking during the test, Timmy."

It is Mr. Jenkins, our teacher.

"I finished early," I tell Mr. Jenkins. "It was one of your easier exams. And frankly, I feel sorry for Meriwether."

"I don't know what that means, Timmy,

but if you're done early, sit quietly at your desk and read."

I wait until Mr. Jenkins has walked back to his desk and lower my voice.

"Who else is in the group, Rollo?"

He says nothing.

"I'll just keep talking if you don't tell me."

He ignores me.

"At least tell me the name of the treasurer."

Mr. Jenkins raises his head and looks in our direction.

I wait until he looks away.

"Fine," I whisper to Rollo. "Don't say a thing. But it's your fault if it takes me forever to solve what might otherwise be an open-and-shut case. And who will YIP YAP blame for that? It won't be me. I'm guessing it will be their sergeant-at-arms."

Rollo looks up at me.

"Don't worry," I tell him. "I'm sure colleges won't care if your application says, 'Disgraced sergeant-at-arms booted from office.'"

Rollo frantically tears off a corner of his exam and scribbles a name on it.

He checks to be sure Mr. Jenkins is not watching and slides me the piece of paper.

"Here," he whispers between gritted teeth. *"It's the treasurer's name. Now . . . be . . . quiet."*

I glance at the torn piece of paper.

And am immediately aware.

It *is* an open-and-shut case.

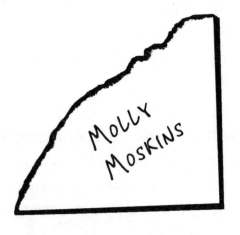

CHAPTER
6
The Fish Scales of Justice

Molly Moskins is the country's most wanted criminal.

But you already know that if you have read any of my prior works.

Molly has stolen shoes, globes, spoons, nature reports, and the sacred honor of the criminal justice system.

For while I have caught her red-handed, she has yet to be criminally prosecuted.

It is a travesty of immense proportion.

But what is worse is that she smells like a tangerine.

Here. Smell for yourself:

"SCRATCH AND SNIFF" MOLLY
(It only works if after you scratch it, you pretend you can smell a tangerine.)

She is a criminal without conscience. A sinner without scruples. A hoodlum without a hood.

← No hood

She would steal the fur from a bear. The scales from a fish. And a fish from a scale.

FRESH FISH

And given access to a charity's hard-earned funds, she would rob it not only blind but deaf.

And deaf is what I will be when Molly Moskins stops yelling.

CHAPTER 7

E-Z Dazed and Confused

"OH, TIMMY! THIS WILL BE THE MOST SPLENDIFEROUS SPRING BREAK VACATION I'VE EVER TAKEN!

I am standing in the parking lot of the E-Z Daze Motel, and the felon herself is jumping up and down next to me.

You heard right.

My mother's caravan-to-nowhere not only involves moving Doorman Dave halfway across the country. It also involves vacationing with her new best friend.

Esther Moskins.

ESTHER MOSKINS (always on smartphone)

Esther is the mother of You-Know-Who:

We can go swimming together!!! We can play shuffleboard together!!!!

Supposedly, we are all traveling to a city called Chicago, where we will help Doorman Dave move into his new apartment. Then Doorman Dave and I and my inconsiderate mother and the tangerine-scented felon and all of the felon's family will vacation together in Chicago.

Oh, did I fail to mention the rest of the felon's family?

Then here, meet them.

This is Mr. Moskins:

MR. MOSKINS

He is Molly's dad. And I know only one thing about him:

He likes maps.

And then there's Molly's little brother, Micah. But she doesn't call him Micah. She calls him this:

I don't want to know why she calls him Snot. I just want to hide from Molly.

So I lock myself in the car.

"Don't you want to come out and play?" asks the tangerine-scented girl.

"We're not staying, Molly Moskins. My mom just pulled the car over because I was fighting with my business partner."

Molly starts to ask me something but is interrupted by the *CLICK-CLICK* of the car doors unlocking.

"What are you doing?" I ask my mom as she gets into the car.

"I'm unlocking the car. So I can get into it. Which is how I drive."

"Are we leaving?" I ask.

"Yes," she says.

"Oh, thank God," I answer.

She rolls down the front passenger window

and leans out toward Molly. "You better go back with your parents, dear. We're not staying here."

Molly runs off.

"Oh, please," I mutter to my mother. "The girl hardly merits a 'dear.' Need I recite her litany of crimes? She probably stole your car stereo while you were yapping."

My mother turns to me in the backseat.

"Seriously, Timmy. Behave. Or else I'm going to pull over the car again and make you go the rest of the way in Dave's car."

Dave's car has no air-conditioning. And that alone is perilous to an Arctic mammal. So for Total's sake, I behave.

Besides, my mother is stressed.

And soon to be more stressed.

"Oh, don't tell me," she says as she turns the key in the ignition and hears nothing.

"No, no, no, don't die on me now," she tells the rental car. "Not here. Not now."

But the car doesn't listen.

Then she says many words that cannot be included here.

And soon all the adults are gathered outside our dead car.

"You guys go on," my mother tells the Moskins family. "Dave and I will wait for the tow truck."

"That could take a day or two," says Esther Moskins, looking up from her smartphone. "We're in the middle of nowhere."

"I'm sure it won't take that long," says Doorman Dave. "We'll be fine."

"We could take Timmy with us if you want," offers Mrs. Moskins. "Show him around Chicago. Probably be more fun for him than being stuck here."

"No, it won't. No, it won't. No, it won't," I interject, contemplating the epic tragedy of traveling with Molly Moskins.

"Timmy," my mom snaps at me.

"That's very nice of you, Esther," says Doorman Dave. "But we don't want to trouble you."

"It's no trouble," says Esther Moskins. "Molly would love to spend time with Timmy!"

Molly smiles.

I am horrified.

"I'll tell you what," says Esther. "Why don't we all spend the night here at the E-Z Daze, and if by tomorrow morning the tow truck hasn't come, we can take Timmy with us to Chicago and you can meet us there later."

"The tow truck will come! The tow truck will come!" I chant.

My mother covers my mouth with her hand.

"You're very sweet, Esther," says my mother. "Let's wait and see what happens with the tow truck. In the meantime, spending the night here might not be a bad idea. At least it will break up the drive."

A condemned man, I exit the vehicle, my only hope a wayward tow truck in the valley of Nowhere.

With no one to turn to, I look up at the neon man on the E-Z Daze sign. And he looks much too happy to be sleeping at the E-Z Daze Motel.

Clearly, he wasn't facing a trip to Chicago with this person:

CHAPTER 8

Ice Ice Total

Total and I are sharing a sofa bed in my mom's motel room.

And he spends no time on it.

Because he has found his happy place just down the hall.

Pity the poor E-Z Daze guest who wants ice and finds a fifteen-hundred-pound polar bear.

Now while it may be hard to believe, there was a point in time when Total was the most reliable business partner a detective could have.

He made the coffee.

He did the filing.

And he did the billing.

But at some point something changed, and when he made one mistake too many, I had no ~~ice~~ but to let him go.

And that is when Total turned to the fine print of our partnership agreement to point out language that I do not remember being there in the first place:

TOTAL FAILURE PARTNERSHIP AGREEMENT

Paragraph 15: Termination.

In the event the Arctic mammal is terminated from his partnership, he shall be entitled to receive one week's pay. AND AS MAYNY BONBONS AS HE KAN EET FOR THE REST OF HISS LIFE AND A NICE COMFEE BED AND HE KAN HAFF WHATEFFER HE WANTS!!!!

I suspect the contract has been altered. But I cannot prove it.

And so Total is now in a better position than he was when he was working. And Failure, Incorporated, is spending more money on bonbons than it brings in.

It is a financial arrangement that cannot continue.

But for now, I must endure my unfortunate fate.

Just like the E-Z Daze guest who wants ice.

And the guests relaxing outside.

By Total's *other* happy place.

CHAPTER 9

The Doorman Always Knocks Once

Doorman Dave knocks on my half-open motel door.

"You coming to dinner, Mr. Failure?" he asks.

I like that he calls me that.

It is a sign of respect.

And it maintains a certain professional distance between me and the man who used to be my doorman.

"Will Molly Moskins be there?" I ask.

"Probably," he says. "I assume she eats food, too."

I consider that. And the fact that when she is in prison, she will be given her meals for free.

"Can I come in?" he asks.

"The door's open," I answer.

He walks in and sits in the chair by the small table. And looks around the worn E-Z Daze room.

"I didn't see you by the pool," he says.

"Molly was there," I answer.

"Shuffleboard?" he asks.

"Molly was there."

"I sense a pattern," he says.

He plays with the TV remote on the table.

"Well, you can sit by me at dinner if you want," he offers.

"What for?" I ask.

"We can get crayons and draw funny pictures of everyone on the back of the place mats," he answers.

I imagine what I would draw.

MOLLY WITH Horse head

by TIMMY FAILURE

Doorman Dave leans forward and lowers his voice. "And besides, it's either that or I have to talk to Mr. Moskins about maps."

"I heard that," my mom says, stepping into the room.

She looks pretty.

So I tell her.

"You didn't have to get all dressed up for dinner at the E-Z Daze Motel, you know."

"I'm not all dressed up. But thank you for the compliment. If it was one."

"And I'll second it," says Doorman Dave.

He kisses her on the cheek. She puts her arms around his waist.

I walk past both of them out the door.

And safely down the hall, I turn and call back to Doorman Dave.

"You can draw your own pictures."

CHAPTER
10
They Say It's Snot's Birthday

At dinner, it becomes clear that not everything Mr. Moskins says is about maps. As I record on a series of place mats:

I get to hear all of this joyless indoctrination because Mr. Moskins is sitting next to me.

And on the other side of me is Molly's little brother, Snot.

And it is Snot's birthday.

So the restaurant gives him a birthday hat and gives the rest of us paper crowns. Though I don't know why. And my mother makes me wear mine.

That's about the only time she's spoken to me. Because she's spent the rest of the time yapping with Mrs. Moskins. The two of them are having quite the time.

So I interrupt them.

"King Timmy wants to know if you've heard from the tow-truck people."

My mom gives me a look and then turns back toward Mrs. Moskins. "Excuse me for a minute, Esther."

"Did you hear from the tow-truck guy?" I repeat.

"No, Timmy."

"Do you want me to call?"

"No."

"Is it time to go back to our room?"

My mother leans down, her face in mine.

"Timmy, you're being rude. Now go talk to Micah."

"Snot."

"What did you say?"

"They call him Snot."

"Don't be gross, Timmy."

I look back at Snot. He is writing his name on the table.

No one says anything to Snot. But Mr. Moskins does talk to his other child.

So I take an extra piece of cake and walk outside, where I find my business partner.

In his third happy place.

"Cake?" I ask.

His large head lunges toward me and swallows the piece whole.

Then he stares at me. Sad.

"What now?" I ask. "That's all the extra cake there was, you greedy malcontent. We're in the middle of nowhere, you know."

But I can see it's not the cake.

So I go back inside the restaurant.

And bring him what he wants.

CHAPTER 11

Dancing King

Alone with Total under the glow of the E-Z Daze man, I hear music.

"Oh, great," I complain. "How am I going to go to sleep tonight with all that racket?"

And then I hear another racket.

"Want to dance?"

It is the far-too-chirpy-for-this-late-at-night voice of Molly Moskins.

"Oh, please, Molly Moskins. What is going *on* in that restaurant?" I ask.

"It's fun. They have a flamenco guitar player. Your parents and my parents seem like they're having a good time."

"*My* parents? Doorman Dave is not my parent, Molly Moskins. He is a doorman my mother is dating. Well, *was* dating. Because now we are moving him to a city far away. And the sooner we can get him there, the sooner

I can return to a detective business that is suffering grievously from my absence."

She smiles and sits down on the curb next to me.

And taps her feet to the music coming from the restaurant.

"Rollo Tookus says you think I stole all the money."

Her abrupt change of topic surprises me.

"You know," she adds, "the money from YIP YAP."

"Stop right there," I say, holding up my index finger. *"Stop right there, Molly Moskins."*

"What's wrong?"

"If this is a confession, I need to read you your Carmen Miranda rights."

"Ooh. What are those?"

"It's something I have to say to you before you blab. Otherwise, I think something bad happens."

"How exciting," she says.

I fumble through my detective log and find the words I'd written down in the back in the event I ever had to formally charge Molly Moskins with a crime.

"Okay," I tell her, "here it is."

"'You have the right to remain silent,'" I read aloud from my detective log. "'And except for your confession, you should always remain silent, because you talk too much and it's very annoying.'"

"Is that it?" she asks.

"I think so," I answer.

"So now what?"

"So now you confess."

"Okay," she says.

"Okay what?"

"Okay, I stole all the money."

The music from the restaurant comes to a sudden stop, as though even the flamenco guy has been stunned.

"All right, all right, slow down," I tell Molly as I grab for my pen.

"The money's right here," she says, holding out five twenty-dollar bills. "Here, count it."

I take the money from her hand.

"Okay, Molly Moskins. Start talking. I want to know everything that happened."

"Okay," she says. "But first, we dance."

"We *what*?"

"First, we dance," she chirps.

"Absurd!" I retort.

"You don't like to dance?"

"Molly Moskins, you have just confessed to a felony that could put you in the big house for the rest of your life! It is hardly the time to dance. And besides, I am the arresting detective! Do you have any idea how that would look to the general public?"

"I won't tell anyone."

"Molly, *NO*. I am not going to dance with a known criminal."

"But you look so handsome in your crown."

"Oh, my God," I cry, smacking my forehead. "People can *hear* you, Molly. My *partner* can hear you."

I look over at Total. He is doing his best to not hear us.

"Molly Moskins, we are going to march back into that restaurant and I am going to call the police and we are going to end your felonious reign of terror."

She shakes her head.

"Why are you shaking your head?" I ask.

And like the cunning felon she is, she springs upon me, grabbing me around the waist.

"AHHH!" I cry. "What are you doing? What are you doing?"

"We're dancing," she answers.

With her hair in my face, my nostrils are overwhelmed by creeping tendrils of tangerine.

I contemplate calling for help.

For back-up.

And in the corner of my eye, I spot Total.

Who once again is doing his best to respect my privacy.

So I am trapped.

At the mercy of a merciless felon.

Whose only goal is to humiliate an officer of the law.

"You'll regret this," I tell her, my arms pinned to my side.

She hums in my ear and rests her head on my chest.

"It's so wonderful," she says.

I close my eyes, for fear I will be recognized by someone. My logic being that if I can't see them, they can't see me.

"Look at the stars," she says, far too close to my ear. "It's so romantic! Like Rome! Or Paris! We should travel somewhere together, Timmy! I have my own debit card, you know."

I squirm, but it is no use. She is an experienced felon and has been abusing the justice system for as long as she has walked.

"I AM DANCING WITH TIMMY FAILURE!" she yells to the half-empty motel parking lot.

"I'm Timmy Fiminal!" I yell. "Timmy FIMINAL!"

"Who?" she asks, still swaying from side to side.

"It's another detective!" I yell to anyone who might hear. "Another detective who is definitely NOT Timmy Failure."

And suddenly the music ends.

Molly lets go, steps back, and smiles.

"There. Was that so bad?" she asks.

"It was worse than bad. It was tragic. It was epically tragic."

She laughs. "You just don't like dancing," she says.

It is more than a detective can take. And I snap.

"No, Molly Moskins! I just don't like dancing with *you*!"

Molly stares at me with her big mismatched pupils.

And runs back inside the restaurant.

Watching her go, I feel a slight sting.

For detectives are tough men. But decent men.

And even felons have feelings.

I contemplate following her back into the restaurant. But I don't.

For as a detective, I know to let the sins of the night be forgiven by the bright light of morning.

So I sit back down on the curb, under the neon glow of the E-Z Daze man.

Who right now looks far from forgiving.

CHAPTER
12
Yippity Yap, Don't Drop That

"We can talk for as long as you want," I tell Rollo. "I'm on the phone in my motel room."

"I think they charge money for that," answers Rollo.

"The phone's *in the room*, Rollo. They can't charge for something that's in the room. It'd be like charging money for the bottles of water on the table."

"Timmy, those are like six dollars each."

I glance at the now empty bottles.

"Listen, Rollo, I didn't call you to talk about bottled water. I called to tell you I solved the case."

"Which case?"

"YIP YAP."

"You solved YIP YAP?"

"Yep."

"Yep, YIP YAP?"

"YIP YAP. Yep."

"I am so confused," says Rollo.

"The stolen treasury," I bark. "I solved the whole thing."

"That was quick."

"I know. The bill is in the mail. And pay promptly. I'd hate to have my bear shake you down."

"So who did it?" asks Rollo.

"Molly Moskins. She confessed to the whole thing."

"She did?"

"Of course she did. That criminal mastermind is finally finished."

"That's surprising," says Rollo.

"What's surprising?"

"That it was Molly."

"Rollo, the girl commits half the crimes in the country. Only a fool would be surprised by—"

There is a loud crash.

I look up and see that Total has dropped the mini-fridge.

"*See* what happens?" I shout at my bear. "*See* what happens when you do that?"

The motel stocks the mini-fridge with candy bars, nuts, and soda. All of which Total ate. So every few minutes, he turns the fridge upside down and shakes it to make sure he hasn't missed anything.

Only now he has dropped it.

"What's going on?" asks Rollo over the phone.

"It's my former business partner. He ate everything in the mini-fridge, and now he's broken it."

"Oh, they definitely charge for the stuff in the mini-fridge," says Rollo. "Not to mention the broken refrigerator."

"Did you hear that?" I shout at the bear. "You've ruined us!"

Embarrassed, Total hides.

"So what's so surprising about Molly Moskins committing another crime?" I ask Rollo.

"Oh, yeah, I was gonna tell you that."

"So tell me."

"Well, it's really weird."

"Say it, Rollo."

Rollo clears his throat.

"Nunzio Benedici confessed to the whole thing."

Before I can react, there is a second loud crash.

But this time, it's not Total.

CHAPTER 13

Keep Your Ear on the Cup

The sound is from the next room. And it sounds like an ice chest has dropped.

I can hear the scooping up of ice. Followed by voices.

I know all this because I am using my high-tech listening device.

A CUP

I hear two people. One of them is my mom. She is yammering about something.

The other is a man. It is not Mr. Moskins. I know this because he is not talking about maps.

Then I hear "Chicago" and "job."

And applying my oversized brain, I realize the second voice is Doorman Dave.

Then the two of them talk about other stuff.

So I grab a motel notepad and write down everything I hear.

E-Z Daze Motel

Mom says,

DOORMAN DAVE Says,

CHAPTER 14

As Chapters Go, One of the Shorter Ones

I know, I know.

You want to know why I cut all that stuff out of the memo at the end of the last chapter.

Well, first off, my mother deserves her privacy. She's a civilian, and she didn't *ask* to be the mother of a world-famous detective.

And second, you don't have to know everything.

And third, it wasn't important.

Really.

Though what happens next is.

CHAPTER 15

What Happens Next

"I've boarded up the door!" I shout.

"You WHAT?" yells my mother from outside our motel room.

"I've boarded up the door!" I repeat.

"You didn't."

"I did," I reply. "The bear's out of control. So I've trapped him in here with me."

"Timmy, open this door right now!" shouts my mother.

"I can't," I answer. "The wood I found in the motel's maintenance shed is quite solid. It won't budge."

"You *really* boarded up the door?!"

"Why do you make it sound like a negative?" I reply. "I'm preventing the bear from causing more damage. He's already broken the mini-fridge, you know."

I hear what sounds like the pounding of her fist upon the outside of the motel door.

"Timmy, tell me this is a joke," she shouts. "Tell me you didn't really nail the door shut!"

"Detectives don't joke, Mother. I boarded up the door. And I'd call that pretty responsible on my part."

"Responsible? How is that responsible?"

"Because if it weren't boarded up, that polar bear would have pushed the ice machine into the pool by now. And besides, being trapped in here gives me time to focus on the YIP YAP case."

"The *what*?" she cries, pounding on the door again.

"The YIP YAP case. There was a confession. Two confessions, really. It's all very strange."

I hear footsteps outside the door, followed by voices.

"He boarded up the door," says my mother.

"He did *what*?" answers a man's voice, followed by more pounding on the door, this time heavier.

"Timmy, this is Dave. Please open up the door."

"Oh, goodness," I reply. "This is getting repetitive. The door is boarded up, Dave."

"We should have just let him go to Chicago with the Moskins," I hear Dave mutter to my mother. *"Now look what he's done."*

"I'm not going to Chicago with the Moskins," I yell through the door.

"How was I supposed to know he'd barricade a motel-room door?" barks my mother to Dave.

"I'm not going to Chicago with the Moskins," I repeat.

"He's a kid!" Dave replies to my mother. "In the middle of nowhere. Kids get bored!"

"Oh, for heaven's sake!" cries my mother. "Listen to me, Timmy. You stand far away from that door. We're going to get someone from the motel to pry it open."

"I'm not going to Chicago with the Moskins," I repeat.

"I'm not kidding around, Timmy," she says. "Are you standing away from the door?"

"I'm not going to Chicago with the Moskins," I answer.

CHAPTER
16
Mother Doesn't Listen

I'm going to Chicago with the Moskins.

For as fate would have it, the Moskins were not thrilled with their E-Z Daze accommodations and wanted to leave. (I'm guessing Esther Moskins did not like the poor reception her beloved smartphone got in the middle of nowhere.)

So while I am no longer in Nowhere-ville, I am now someplace worse.

In the backseat of a car, bookended by my two favorite people.

And it's an uncomfortable place to be.
Because Molly is not speaking to me.

And Snot *is* speaking to me.

And Esther Moskins is singing sanitized road songs.

And Mr. Moskins is saying things about roads.

It is as though my vengeful mother has calculated exactly how to make me the most uncomfortable traveler on our country's highway system.

Or at least the second most uncomfortable.

CHAPTER
17
Ironing Board Butterfly

"It's a lie-detector test," I tell Molly Moskins.

"It sounds exciting," she answers.

It is a rainy morning in Chicago. I am stuck in a hotel room with Molly Moskins. She is in a better mood than in the car, so I am using the opportunity to get to the bottom of the now messy YIP YAP case.

"What do I do?" she asks.

"Well, first I tie this string to your finger. Then I ask you a question. And when you answer, you pull the string."

"All right," she says.

"Okay," I tell her. "Did you, Molly Moskins, steal YIP YAP's money?"

She giggles.

"You can't giggle, Molly Moskins. This is a felony investigation."

"Okay," she says. "Ask me again."

"Did you, Molly Moskins, steal YIP YAP's money?"

"Yes," she answers, and pulls the string.

"The cow says MOOOOOO," says the lie-detector equipment.

"What's that mean?" asks Molly.

"I think it means you're lying," I answer.

"Let's do it again," says Molly.

I reset the lie-detector machine by turning the farmer in the center to twelve o'clock.

"Okay, get ready," I say. "Did you, Molly Moskins, steal YIP YAP's money?"

"No," she answers, and pulls the string.

"The cow says MOOOOOO," says the lie detector.

"You can't say 'No,'" I tell her. "You just said 'Yes' to the exact same question!"

"I changed my mind," she says.

"But you handed me the stolen money at the E-Z Daze Motel!"

"That might have been my brother's birthday money," she whispers. "Or it might have not."

"Make up your mind, Molly Moskins!" I tell her. "Did you steal the money or not?"

"Well, the machine doesn't seem to know the difference. It says I was lying both times."

Of course.

She is using psychological gamesmanship

to outwit the machine. It is shrewdly calculating. Boldly devious. And it is precisely what separates her from the common criminal.

"Let's take a break," I tell her.

"Okay," she says. "We should probably play with You-Know-Who, anyway."

"You-Know-Who" being her little brother, Snot.

Who is currently standing on the ironing board.

"What's he doing?" I ask Molly.

"I don't know," she answers.

And that's when I see the pen in his hand.

"I think he's trying to write his name on the ceiling," I tell Molly.

"Micah, NO!" she says, running toward him.

Seeing her approach, Snot sprints down the length of the ironing board like it's an Olympic springboard, leaps off the end, and yells something that sounds like:

"INO WUD DADOO MINSES!"

I have no idea what it means, or if he even said it. He might have been reciting the Pledge of Allegiance for all I know.

But I do know that as he said it, Mr. Moskins walked into the room.

And I do know the result of the dive:

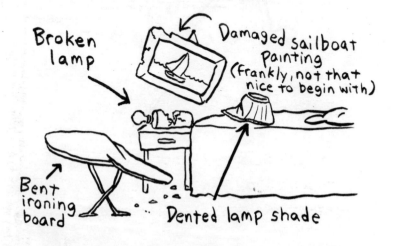

Broken lamp

Damaged sailboat painting (frankly, not that nice to begin with)

Bent ironing board

Dented lamp shade

And oh, yeah.

One more result, too:

CHAPTER 18

Bye, Bye, Rollo— The Telephone Hour

"Meriwether Lewis and William Clark were two explorers who President Thomas Jefferson sent to explore the Louisiana Purchase and find a water route to the Pacific Ocean. They traveled from St. Louis to what is now Oregon with their Shoshone guide Sacagawea and . . ."

"You're boring me," I tell Rollo.

I am on the free hotel phone making calls during Molly's absence, and Rollo is talking about a man named Meriwether.

"Well, I saw the grade you got on Mr. Jenkins's history test, and it wasn't very good," says Rollo.

"Oh, please, Rollo. Grades matter to normal people. I am not a normal people."

"Normal *person*," Rollo corrects me.

"That does it. I'm hanging up."

"Don't hang up."

"Well, then stop wasting my time. I've had a trying couple of days and my nerves are shot. If you have something to say, say it."

"It wasn't Nunzio."

"What wasn't Nunzio?"

"The person who stole the YIP YAP money. It wasn't Nunzio."

"You said he confessed! What's happening over there? It's like the whole town falls apart when I'm gone!"

"Well, I guess Nunzio was talking to Max Hodges the other day, and Nunzio said . . ."

"But when Max Hodges was talking to Jimmy Weber, Max told him that Nunzio said . . ."

"And when Jimmy Weber was talking to Gunnar, it became . . ."

"And when Gunnar was discussing it with Mr. Jenkins, it turned into . . ."

"And when Mr. Jenkins mentioned it to me, I could have sworn he said . . ."

"That's it!" I tell Rollo.

"What's it?"

"Nunzio!" I shout. "He's molding all the bunnies."

"No, Timmy, you—"

"Now the only question is *why*!"

"Timmy, Nunzio wasn't—"

"Stop talking, Rollo. I need to *think*."

But I can't.

Because there's an interruption at the hotel door.

CHAPTER 19

Rainy Days and Mothers Always Get Me Down

It's Mr. Moskins, and he's holding a cell phone.

"It's your mother, Tim."

It's as though she has radar for when detective work needs to be interrupted.

I take the phone from Mr. Moskins.

"Hello, Mother. I'm very busy."

"Hi, sweetheart. How are you?"

"Busy," I repeat. "My Chicago work has me swamped."

"Well, I just called to say the car is fixed. The tow-truck man was able to do the repairs himself. So we should be there early this afternoon."

"There's no rush," I answer.

"Don't get so excited," she says. "Are you going to do anything with the Moskins today?"

"It's raining, Mother. There's nothing we can do."

"Oh, Timmy, it's a big city. Maybe you can go to a museum."

"A museum?" I snap. "Mother, I'm in the middle of an investigation that's taken me halfway across the continent. I have conflicting reports from eyewitnesses. I have a bear who's eating my profits. I have a roommate who's a felon. And I'm with a family that—"

I see Mr. Moskins standing at the end of the hall.

I lower my voice.

"I'm with a family that makes *ours* look ideal."

"Timmy," she says, "be nice. That was very kind of them to take you to Chicago."

"Kind?" I answer. "It was torture."

"Why don't we talk about this when I get there?"

"Fine. But my appointment book is full all next week."

"We'll talk about this when I get there, Timmy. Hand the phone to Mr. Moskins."

"Okay. But don't go giving him any ideas about things to do in Chicago. I'm strapped for time as it is."

"Hand the phone to Mr. Moskins," she repeats.

So I hand the phone to Mr. Moskins and go back into the hotel room and shut the door.

And there's another knock.

From Mr. Moskins again.

And he looks much too excited about the thing he says next.

"Tim, we're going to a museum!"

CHAPTER 20

Grant Wood Not Like This

I know nothing about art.

But if my mother is going to punish me by furthering my misery with the Moskins, I am going to make the most of it.

So when we get to the museum, I hand the museum woman my business card.

Failure, Inc.
(not as bad as it sounds)

"What is this?" she asks.

"I'm Timmy Failure," I answer.

"Okay," she says.

"This is in case your art is ever stolen," I add.

She stares at the card.

"I wrote my number on the back. It's the Timmyline. Call anytime. But if a bear answers, hang up. He's not supposed to be answering the phone."

"Enjoy the museum," she says.

I walk through the turnstile and see Mr. Moskins on the other side.

He is studying a map.

"Okay," he says, talking to no one. "If we walk down this center hall, we can make a left at the end and see the Modern wing. Then we'll circle clockwise to cover the rest of this floor. Then we can go up these stairs over here to the next floor and circle it in the same clockwise fashion. How does that sound?"

He looks up absentmindedly.

"Have you seen Micah?" he asks.

I haven't. Which means that by now he has destroyed something.

"Oh, God," I say, pointing at a sculpture. "He's torn the arms off that statue."

Mr. Moskins smiles and points to a photo of the sculpture on his map.

"No arms there, either," he says.

We continue our walk down the main hall until we get to a large gallery. And see Snot.

With a museum map wrapped around his head.

"INO WUD DADOO MINSES," he yells—
his incomprehensible babble of choice.

I remove the map from his head.

"TIMMYYYY!" he shouts in my face.

"We've been looking everywhere for you,"
says his father. "Where have you been?"

Snot holds up a pen and the unrolled
museum map.

He has written his name all over it.

"Your name is Micah," his dad says to him, and then turns to me. "His sister gave him that nickname. Drives his mother and me crazy. Now he thinks it *is* his name."

He takes Micah's map and folds it up so the writing can't be seen. And he turns to me again.

"About earlier today," he adds, "I'm sorry you had to see all that, Tim. Molly just needs to learn to be responsible. That's why I asked her to stay at the hotel with her mother. She can see the museum another time."

I don't say anything. But I know the real reason they asked her to stay home:

She is a felon.

And she would steal every piece of art her brother didn't break.

We continue our tiresome walk through the museum. And find a painting of a farmer and his wife.

"This is called . . . *American Gothic*," says Mr. Moskins, checking the museum brochure to be sure. "It's very famous."

"Why?" I ask.

"Because it's on the brochure," says Mr. Moskins. "They only put the famous ones on the brochure."

I stare at the painting.

"I think he killed a man," I say.

"Who killed a man?" asks Mr. Moskins.

"The farmer. And he did it with that pitchfork."

A museum guide overhears me.

"This painting is not about a murder," the guide interrupts. "It represents—"

"She had her suspicions about the old guy when she married him," I add, pointing to the farmer's wife. "Who wouldn't? I mean, look at his criminal face."

The museum guide rubs his eyes.

"And now the wife knows what he did," I continue. "The wife knows *everything*. That's why she's staring so nervously at the pitchfork."

The guide starts to talk, but I stop him.

"So now the old farmer is thinking, *Maybe*

I've got to get rid of her, too."

"Okay. That's all I can take," says the guide.

"Please, sir, I'm a detective. I know what I'm talking about. My only question for you is, Has this man been arrested?" I point at the man in the painting.

"It is a *painting*," he says slowly. "He is not *real*."

"I thought the same thing about Meriwether," I answer.

"Who?" he asks.

"Meriwether Lewis. The man Clark made fun of."

"What does Meriwether Lewis have to do with Grant Wood?" he asks.

"Who is Grant Wood?" I answer.

"The man who painted this," answers the guide. "Which I'm afraid shows how much you know about this painting."

I smile.

"It shows how much *you* know about the painting," I answer, staring down at the placard, where the painter's typed name has been crossed out and written in with pen.

I point down at the placard.

"It was painted by this fellow."

American Gothic, 1930
Oil on Beaver Board
30 ¾" x 25 ¾"

Artist: ~~Wood Grant~~ **SNOT**

CHAPTER 21

The King and I

You're probably wondering why I haven't mentioned the polar bear in a while.

That's because ever since he got his paper crown in the E-Z Daze parking lot, he has come to believe he is an actual king.

So now he spends his entire day in the crown and a hotel bathrobe.

The robe has small gold letters embossed on the breast pocket. The letters are "HH."

I don't know what the letters stand for. But I do know how Total has chosen to interpret them.

All that would be bad enough.

But then the bear discovered room service.

Now I'm pretty sure that like the telephone, all the food here is free.

But if it isn't, somebody is going to get a very large bill.

And that bill may also include something that I'm pretty sure *does* cost money:

Pay-per-view television.

Because that fat bear is ordering one television show after another.

Cooking shows.

Talk shows.

Soap operas.

And his new favorite:

So now Total doesn't leave the room. And the room doesn't get cleaned.

Because no housekeeper wants to spend an extended amount of time with an omnivorous polar bear.

I've tried to explain to the hotel's housekeeping staff that the polar bear is well fed. And that as such, he is not likely to eat a person.

NOT LIKELY

But they are not reassured.

But it's all academic now.

Because like it or not, King Total's reign is about to be brought to a crushing end.

By a tyrant who weighs a lot less than he does.

CHAPTER 22

The Icewoman Cometh

"Well, hello, stranger," my mother says, hugging me in the hotel hallway.

"I just finished moving Dave's stuff into his new apartment," she says. "You should see his view. He can practically see all of Lake Michigan."

"Did you say good-bye to him?" I ask. "Thank him for the memories?"

My mother smiles.

"No, I didn't say good-bye. He's coming back here to the hotel after he unpacks some more boxes. He wants to spend time with all of us this afternoon."

"So where am I staying?" I ask.

"In my hotel room. With me. It's one floor up from here."

"But I'm already sharing a room with Molly and Snot. It's attached to Mr. and Mrs. Moskins's room."

"Don't call him Snot, Timmy. His name is Micah. But sure, you can stay with them if you want."

"Then I want to stay with them."

"That's fine," she says, hugging me again. "I just thought we could stay up late. Maybe even get room service. If the hotel has it."

"Oh, *they have it*," I answer. "But I'll stay with Molly tonight."

"Are you sure?"

"I'm sure. The girl is a flight risk."

"Is that so?"

"Please, Mother. Don't you remember the

last time we left her alone? She fled to Peru."[3]

"Okay, Timmy. You keep an eye on Molly. But keep a spot on your dance card open for me today."

"I don't dance, Mother."

"It's just an expression, Timmy. It means save some time for me today. I was hoping to talk to you."

I hear the phone ring in my hotel room.

I run to answer it, and as I do, I yell back to my mother.

"Sorry, Mom. *Dance card full!*"

---

3. A reference to my third masterpiece, *Timmy Failure: We Meet Again*. If you have not read it, shame on you.

CHAPTER 23
You Have the Right to Remain Rollo

"What now?" I ask Rollo.

"I forgot to tell you something," he answers.

"Events are moving rapidly, Rollo. It better be good."

"It *is* good. It's about the last YIP YAP meeting. The last one before the theft. I saw someone there. Now, I don't think—"

"Wait a minute," I interrupt. "*You* saw someone there. What were *you* doing there?"

"No, Timmy, that's not the point. The point is—"

"Rollo Tookus, I am in the midst of a cross-country investigation that's left a trail of exorbitant hotel bills, and you surprise me with that fact *now*?"

"I haven't said anything yet."

"You just admitted you were at the last meeting of YIP YAP before the theft."

"I'm the sergeant-at-arms! So what?"

"So being at that meeting makes you a suspect."

"Me?" chimes Rollo. "Why would I steal funds meant for some poor Yergi Plimkin kid?"

"You tell me," I answer. "Maybe you wanted his books. And if you're about to confess, tell me now, because I'll need to read you your Carmen Miranda rights."

"'Miranda' rights, Timmy. Not '*Carmen* Miranda' rights. Carmen Miranda was a singer with fruit on her head."

Carmen Miranda (according to Rollo)

"Calm down, Rollo. You're being very defensive."

"And you're being crazy. Timmy, I'm the person that YIP YAP asked to *find* the stolen money."

"Perfect cover, isn't it?"

"But I would never steal anything!" protests Rollo.

"Interesting," I answer. "And who took the Miracle report from Mr. Jenkins's storage cupboard? The paper that every student in the class wanted to cheat off?"[4]

---

4. Another reference to my famed third volume, *Timmy Failure: We Meet Again*. You really need to read that book.

"My taking the Miracle report was an accident!"

"You better stop talking now, Rollo Tookus. Or I'm going to have to read you your rights. With or without fruit on your head."

There is a loud wail.

"What was that?" asks Rollo.

"My polar bear. I think he just ran out of *Real Housewives* episodes.

"I've got to go, Rollo. The forsaken beast could tear up the entire room."

I hang up the phone and watch as Total grabs the bedsheet and covers his head in mourning.

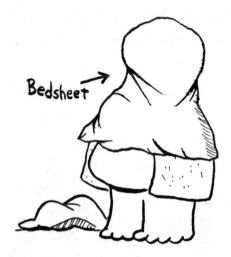

Bedsheet →

On a professional level, I am angry at the bear. He has betrayed the agency and abused our contractual relationship for the sole purpose of attaining a lifetime of creature comforts.

← Bonbons

But on a personal level, I know that he and I have a history together. And a friendship that probably shouldn't have been mixed with business in the first place.

So I calm him down.

And coax him onto the sheetless bed.

And hand-feed him the last of the bonbons.

CHAPTER 24

All the Redemption I Can Offer, Girl, Is Beneath This Dirty Bean

Molly Moskins won't stop jabbering.

"My cousin Mimi is fifteen and she does anything she wants, and we're gonna go see her tomorrow because she lives here in Chicago. She's very bad. I can't wait."

I am forced to listen to her chatter because I am stuck next to her at lunch.

Though it is better than sitting next to Mr. Moskins. And it is better than sitting next to Snot, whose punishment for his museum behavior appears to be eating here, at a pizza joint where writing on the walls is *encouraged*.

And it is better than sitting next to my mother and Doorman Dave, who, with no sense of taste or decency, hold hands with each other while eating.

"And my cousin Mimi has a boyfriend in Denver!" Molly continues. "Can you believe that? Her family says she can't have a boyfriend, but she doesn't tell them, and so they don't know. She even visited him once. Isn't that fantastical?"

She stops talking. It is a relief. Like a cool breeze on a hot summer day.

"What's the matter, Timmy?"

"I'm trying to focus, Molly Moskins."

"On what?"

"On a number of profound things. And I really don't want to hear about your cousin in Denver."

"She's in Chicago. Her boyfriend's in Denver."

"I don't care where he is, Molly Moskins. I just want to think. I'm a detective. It's how I put food on my table."

Reminded of food, Molly eats the last of her pizza crust.

I stare out the window.

And see a park.

"That's Millennium Park," she says. "It's really wonderful. They have concerts there in the summer. And they have a giant silvery bean where you can see your reflection."

GIANT SILVERY BEAN ←

"Okay," she adds, "I'll stop talking now so you can do your detective concentration thing."

I don't answer.

She looks to the other side of her, toward her mother.

"Can I have another slice of pizza?" she asks her mom.

Her mom is doing something on her phone, so she doesn't answer.

But her father does.

"You've had enough, Molly. My goodness. You're not a horse."

And the table grows suddenly quiet.

Save for the sound of Mr. Moskins's knife cutting his pizza. And the tapping of Mrs. Moskins's fingers upon the screen of her phone. And the scrawl of Snot's pencil across the wall.

And a voice.

"I want to see that bean right now, Molly Moskins!"

It is me, and my mouth has momentarily lost its mind.

Her eyes widen.

"Can I go, Mom?" she pleads. "Can I go? It's right across the street! I'll be with Timmy!"

Her mom looks up from her phone and over to Mr. Moskins, who says nothing.

"Fine, sweetie," she says, looking back down at her phone. "But you two stay together. And stay where we can see you."

"You take good care of Molly," adds my mother.

So we exit the restaurant and Molly is jumping up and down and she is skipping and she is talking.

Talking like there is a countdown to a time of no more words, and she must use them all before the deadline.

But I listen. And listen.

And listen.

For detectives are tough men. But decent men.

And when we approach the giant bean, I escape momentarily to walk underneath it. Where I stare up at the broad curve of its underside.

And see myself.

Stretched tall.

Almost grown.

With strangers from the park around me.

And when Molly finds me under the bean, I interrupt her monologue to say only one thing.

"I want to leave."

CHAPTER
25
Leaving in an Elevator

When we get back to the hotel after lunch, the receptionist says there's a message for our room.

"From a Rollo Tookus," he adds.

"Must be for you," my mother says, Doorman Dave by her side.

"I tried to write down everything he said," says the receptionist, "but some of it was a little hard to understand. I put question marks where I wasn't sure."

He hands me the message.

To: <u>TIMMY FAILURE</u>

From: <u>ROLLO TOOKIS</u> (?)

IMPORTANT MESSAGE

Re: <u>TRied to tell you, but</u>
<u>you didn't listen. At last</u>
<u>meeting of Yippy Yap (?)...</u>
<u>The person I saw there...</u>
<u>It was Corrine (?) Corrina.</u>

"Oh, good God," I shout.

"Are you all right?" asks my mother.

I take a step away and continue reading the note.

<u>Would have asked Corrina</u>
<u>~~questions~~ questions myself, but can't.</u>
<u>Her and dad on spring break</u>
<u>vacation. In some fancy Chicago hotel (?)</u>

"CORRINA CORRINA'S A FUGITIVE FROM JUSTICE!" I declare.

My mother claps her hand over my mouth and hisses, *"Timmy, you are in a hotel lobby. Control yourself."*

The receptionist looks away.

"Mother, I want to go back to my room right now. I need time alone to think!"

"Timmy, you're sharing a room with Molly and Micah. And the Moskins left the restaurant right after us. So I'm sure they are going to be here any min—"

"I'll take any time I can get!" I say, cutting her off.

She takes my hand and walks me toward the elevator. Dave follows behind.

"You don't have to hold my hand," I tell her.

She doesn't let go.

With her other hand, she presses the UP button. And kneels by my side.

"Timmy, I know that you love your detective work. And it's wonderful that you do. But we are going to spend time together and we are going to talk."

The elevator doors open.

"We can talk at home, Mother."

"No, Timmy, here."

The elevator doors begin to close. Doorman Dave holds them open.

"We're gonna miss the elevator, Mother."

"Timmy," she says.

"The doorman is holding the elevator, Mother."

"You have twenty minutes," she tells me. "Then you're going to come back down to the lobby and we're going to talk. Or I'm going to get very angry."

I run inside the elevator.

And push the button for my floor.

And the doors close.

And as I ascend, I look through the clear-glass elevator walls down upon the interior courtyard of the hotel. And down upon my mother and Doorman Dave.

Who slowly recede from my view.

And are gone.

CHAPTER 26

Gumshoe, Burning Down the Avenue

I don't have a lot of time to tell you this next part, so I'm going to be brief.

Corrina Corrina is so evil she could scare the tail off a beaver.

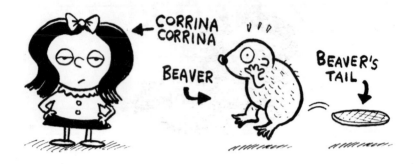

CORRINA CORRINA

BEAVER

BEAVER'S TAIL

She is ruthless and diabolical and cunning and immoral and destructive and secretive and wicked and depraved and malicious and vicious and dishonorable and corrupt and fraudulent and vile and nefarious and sordid and smelly and apparently one time I kissed her.[5]

And with all that said, I'm now running out of time.

So the point is this:

Corrina Corrina stole the money.

---

5. That last part is a claim made by Rollo Tookus. It is a bold and outrageous lie. And if it were true, I would say that it was not true. So either way, you can rest assured it's not true.

THE MONEY

And I will hunt her down and get it back or my name is not Failure.

And that means going wherever she goes.

And so, when my mother got to my hotel room that afternoon . . .

516

. . . She could not get angry with me.

For I was already gone.

CHAPTER
27
Meet the In-Laws

But crosstown manhunts can get lonely.

So just as the explorer Meriwether had Clark . . .

GUY WITH FUNNY NAME

CLARK

and the outlaw Bonnie had Clyde . . .

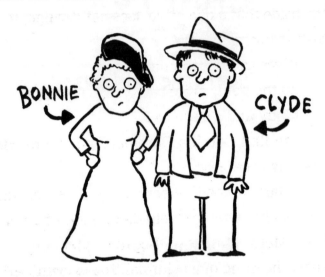

the detective Failure had Moskins.

I will not share the details of (1) why I agreed to bring her or (2) how we escaped on the city bus across town.

And that is because if there is one trick of the trade that a detective does not divulge, it is his method of escape.

Lives can depend on it.

So the point is this:

Molly and I were free.

I to find Corrina Corrina. And she to witness my greatness.

"Many a good detective has relied on unsavory characters to help them find bad guys," I tell Molly Moskins. "Because who better to know the mind of a criminal than a criminal?"

"I know," says Molly. "I can help a *lot*!"

I nod.

"We're like Bonnie and Clyde," she says. "But instead of being outlaws, we're *in*-laws. Or whatever the opposite of outlaws is."

"Yes, Molly. And remember, while our goal is to find the money, our secondary goal is to project greatness. That's how I've branded my detective agency, and that's the message we're going to spread from street to street."

"That's what I was thinking!" adds Molly.

"Now all the intel we have from Rollo is

that Corrina Corrina is staying at some fancy hotel. So we'll have to check every one of them."

"Where do we start?"

"With this one," I say, staring at a brochure I found near the bus stop. "It's called the Drakonian."

"It sounds wonderful!" says Molly.

"Yes," I answer. "But first I need to make a phone call."

CHAPTER
28

Hello, I Love You, Won't You Tell Me Where You Are?

"Hi, it's me, Timmy," I say into the first pay phone we can find.

"Oh, Timmy, I've missed you!" I hear my great-aunt Colander say.

GREAT-AUNT COLANDER

"What's the matter?" I ask. "You sound sick."

"Oh, I'm always sick," she answers. "But what do doctors know? I'm an old woman. Where are you?"

"On the road. With my new associate, Molly Moskins. She's a criminal, but I'm granting her leniency in return for her cooperation."

"Well, good for you, Timmy. Though I'm not sure I know what that means."

"It's detective talk, Aunt Colander. But I don't have much time. And I need to ask you for a favor."

"What is it?"

"Well, since you're sort of an honorary member of my agency, I thought I could trust you with a highly sensitive mission."

"Ooh. Sounds exciting. But what do you need me to do?"

I glance around at the strangers standing near the pay phone and lean in close to the receiver.

"Just tell my mom I'm okay."

She pauses.

"She's not with you?"

"No. But it's fine. I'm with a bunch of people."

A BUNCH OF PEOPLE
(STRANGERS, YES. BUT
STILL PEOPLE.)

"Who are you with?" she asks.

"I have to get back on the bus, Aunt Colander."

"Well, where are you off to?" she asks.

"I have to go."

"Timmy, I—"

"I love you, Aunt Colander! Don't forget the mission! Good-bye!"

I hang up the phone and run with Molly for the bus.

"Why couldn't you just call your mother yourself?" asks Molly as we run.

"*Think*, Molly Moskins."

"I'm not good at thinking," she replies.

We hop onto the bus just before the doors close and take a seat near the back.

I lower my voice.

"Because her phone will be *tapped*, Molly Moskins. That means that if I call, the police will know exactly where I called from."

"Ohhhh," she replies, finally getting it. "And then they'd catch *us* before we could catch Corrina Corrina!"

"Exactly," I reply.

"That would be so unfair!" she declares. "We're the in-laws! The good guys!"

"Yes," I tell her. "It's as though the world's gone mad."

Defiant, she reaches into her backpack and pulls out what looks like an old sweatshirt.

Upon which she has written something.

Something that may not fend off this mad world. But shows we will at least try.

CHAPTER 29
Bear on the Run

We weren't the only ones to flee the hotel room.

For as it turns out, everything you get in a hotel is not free.

The mini-fridge. The room service. The pay-per-view.

All of it costs money.

And when the hotel came to collect the exorbitant bill, my ex-business partner climbed out the window and down the fire escape.

Though how he met us across town is anyone's guess.

I suppose it has something to do with the fact that he's a polar bear. And that a polar bear can sniff out a seal from more than twenty miles away.

And anyone who can do that can certainly find a bus filled with sixty smelly people.

And thus, the three of us were now one.

One of us running from justice. Two of us running to enforce it.

And after a long ride across town, we were just where we needed to be.

CHAPTER 30
The Tears of a Molly

"Welcome to the Drakonian," says the jug-eared doorman. "Can I help you with something?"

"We're looking for a hotel," I respond.

"Well, you found one. Are you here with your parents?"

"No," I answer. "Why would we be?"

"Well, you need to be at least eighteen years old to check into the Drakonian."

Molly Moskins steps forward.

"We're looking for Corrina Corrina," she says.

"Is she a guest at the hotel?" the doorman asks.

"She's a felon," I answer. "And we have no idea where she is."

"She took the money for Yergi Plimkin's books," adds Molly Moskins.

"Who is Yogi Plimkin?" asks the doorman.

"Yergi," answers Molly. "And he's a sad little boy."

SAD LITTLE BOY → YERGI

"And is *he* a guest here?" asks the doorman.

"Negative," I chime in. "The poor kid can't afford books. How is he going to afford a nice hotel like this?"

"I don't know," he answers. "I don't even know who he is."

"Sir, can you please stop going on about Yergi Plimkin?" pleads Molly. "He has no books and you're going to make me cry."

"Oh, please don't," he says, touching Molly on the shoulder. "I don't even know what's going on."

"He doesn't even know what's going on!" howls Molly. *"He doesn't care!"*

And quick as a clap of thunder, she begins bawling.

"Oh, my goodness," says the doorman. "What is happening here?"

"*Now* look what you've done," I scold the doorman. "The little girl's weeping. Is that the job of a doorman? To make little girls weep?"

Strangers begin to gather on the sidewalk.

"I didn't mean anything bad at all," he

assures Molly. "I think it's great you're help-ing this . . . uh, Yergi fellow."

"He said his name *again*!" Molly bellows, convulsing in renewed hysterics.

"What do you think you're *doing*?" I ask the helpless doorman. "*Think* before you talk."

"Oh, my goodness," he says, reaching for an embroidered handkerchief to wipe Molly's tears.

As he does so, the crowd of onlookers grows.

"Don't look now," I caution the doorman, "but your conduct has attracted an angry mob."

He looks over at me.

Molly sobs louder.

"Remain calm," I admonish the doorman. "This mob has vengeance in their eyes."

"Okay," he says to me. "Thank you, but you are really not helping."

Molly wails to the heavens.

"All right, all right," he says, kneeling in front of the now inconsolable Molly. "Why don't we all just step inside the hotel, and the three of us can take a ni-i-i-i-ce comfy seat in the lobby? Then I can get you some water and—"

"Oh, good God," I'm forced to interject, "my associate's on the verge of a nervous breakdown, and all you offer her is *a drink of water*? It's like you're *trying* to inflame the mob."

He turns toward me. "Okay, you are truly not helping the situation, Mr.—"

Molly begins pulling her hair, as though she is trying to yank it out in grief-soaked clumps.

"Failure," I answer, handing him my card. "And as an officer of the law, I will save you despite yourself."

"No, no, please don't," he begins to say, looking down at my card and then back up at me.

But I am no longer there.

For I am high atop his doorman's station. Heroic and noble.

"DO NOT TEAR THIS POOR MAN LIMB FROM LIMB!" I bellow to the surging horde. "THOUGH YOUR CONDUCT WOULD CERTAINLY BE JUSTIFIED!"

But even this fails to calm the un-calmable crowd.

So as the doorman ushers Molly inside the lobby, I rush inside with them. And as I do, I remain level-headed enough to order that the front door of the hotel be guarded by my security detail.

Who is unarmed.

Though not empty-handed.

CHAPTER
31
Suite Dreams Are Made of This

"How long do you think we can stay in here?" asks Molly, now recovered and splayed across the couch of the hotel's largest suite.

"I suppose for as long as our food holds out," I answer, staring at the suite's dining-room table, now piled high with all the candy and soda the hotel's gift shop could give us.

"They let us take everything!" exclaims Molly, grabbing a handful of Hershey's Kisses.

"What did you take, Timmy?"

"All the shaving cream I could grab." I add, "A detective's beard grows in fast."

Molly runs through the suite, her voice echoing like that of a lost yodeler.

"Ooooh, we have a bedroom. . . . And a living room. . . . And a bathroom. . . . And ooooooh, a big closet! . . . And a . . ."

Her voice trails off.

She walks back into the dining room.

"What's a bridal suite?" she asks, staring down at the cover of a brochure.

"Let me see that," I say.

"Don't," she says, pulling it away from me. "You'll get shaving cream on it."

She opens the brochure. It is filled with pictures of happy women in long white gowns.

"Ohhh, *bridal*!" she exclaims. "As in the word *bride*!"

She jumps up and down, flinging the brochure from her hand.

"Oh, Timmy!" she cries. "It's like we're *married*!"

She spins around, ecstatic.

"Let me see that!" I say, picking up the brochure from the floor.

I stare at it and see a photo of a woman in a long white dress. She is with a man in a black tuxedo. And they are both riding a horse.

"Oh, Molly Moskins, don't you understand *anything*?" I yell. "It's a horse!"

She looks at the photo.

"So?" she asks.

"So they don't mean *bridal* as in *bride*. They mean *bridle* as in the thing you use to control a horse."

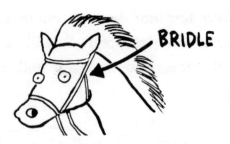

BRIDLE

"Ohhhh," she exclaims, the obvious finally dawning upon her. "Are you sure?"

"Don't insult me, Molly Moskins. I'm sure of everything I say."

She walks into the bedroom and climbs atop the large bed.

"So why's this bed shaped like a heart?" she asks.

I follow her into the bedroom and stare at the giant heart-shaped bed.

"Molly," I mutter, "do I have to spell *this* out, too?"

"I guess so," she says.

"It's because a heart represents love," I explain. "And people *love* horses."

"Ohhhhh," she exclaims again. "I didn't think about that."

She stares at the brochure.

"So what do you do if you have the bridle suite?" she asks.

We exchange glances.

And for once, we are of the same mind.

CHAPTER
32
To Protect and to Sanitize

"We want a horse!" we shout at the housekeeper, both of us slightly delirious from an
overdose of candy.

The housekeeper is standing in the open
doorway of an adjoining room, her housekeeping cart blocking part of the hallway.

"Who are you?" she asks.

"We're in-laws," answers Molly. "Like Bonnie and Clyde, but the opposite."

"Do you have names?" she asks.

"I'm the detective Timmy Failure. And this is the felon Molly Moskins. I am with her only because she has agreed to mend her venal ways and assist in the apprehension of Corrina Corrina."

"Of course," says the housekeeper.

"And we need a horse to help capture her," adds Molly.

"Makes sense," replies the housekeeper, tossing dirty towels into the bag at the end of her cart.

"So are you going to help us get a horse or not?" I ask.

The housekeeper looks up and down the hall. *"Keep your voice down,"* she whispers.

"What for?" asks Molly. "We're staying in the bridle suite. We're entitled to a horse."

The housekeeper leans in close.

"Because I'm Killer Katy Kumquat," she whispers.

I glare warily at the housekeeper.

"Tell us more," I say.

"No," she says.

"Please," I persist.

"I've said too much already," she answers.

"You can confide in us," I assure her. "I give you my word as a man and as a law-enforcement officer."

"I think that's the problem," says the housekeeper.

"What's the problem?" I ask.

"You're a *cop*," she says, her lips dripping with scorn.

"What of it?" I retort. "It is a noble profession."

"Hmmph," she sneers. "I work *outside* the law. For the benefit of everyone."

"Oh, my goodness," exclaims Molly. "Does that mean what I think that means?"

"It means nothing," answers the house-keeper, straightening the tiny shampoo bottles on the top of her cart.

"Oh, my goodness!" Molly exclaims again. "It *does* mean something."

"No, it doesn't," says the housekeeper. "Drop it. Just drop the whole thing."

"I won't drop it! I won't drop it at all!" answers Molly.

"Will someone please tell me what's going on here?" I shout.

Molly grabs me by both shoulders.

"Timmy," she says, pausing with eyes wide open, "Killer Katy's a *crime-fighting superhero*!"

CRIME-FIGHTING SUPERHERO

"Keep your voice down!" the housekeeper hisses.

"Absurd!" I cry.

"Is it true?" Molly asks, tugging on the housekeeper's uniform. "Is it true? Is it true?"

The housekeeper lowers her head. "Perhaps," she mumbles. "But any magical superpowers I have are used only for good. And that's all I'm going to say."

"OH. MY. GOODNESS!" Molly gasps, turning in astonishment to me. "Timmy, she can get us a horse! She can get us a plane! She can get us anything!!"

Molly gets down on her knees and embraces the housekeeper's leg. "My hero!" she cries.

"Okay, okay, hold it right there!" I declare, interrupting the lovefest. "You listen to me, Kumquat, or Killer Katy, or whoever you are. You can fool a naive little girl, but you can't fool a streetwise detective. Now, if you're so magical, *prove it*."

The housekeeper glares at me with contempt.

And then closes her eyes.

"What are you doing?" I ask.

"Hush," she says. "I need to concentrate."

"Concentrate on what?" I ask.

"Right now," she answers, "as the three of us are standing here in this hallway, I'm wrapping a toilet with a paper band."

"Where?" I ask. "What toilet?"

"In the open room behind you," she answers, her eyes still shut.

"What kind of band?" I grill her.

"A paper band," she answers.

"You said 'paper band' already!" I snap. "Now, be *specific*."

The housekeeper pauses.

And then answers.

"A paper band that says SANITIZED FOR YOUR PROTECTION."

I stand motionless.

"Go in there and check," I tell Molly, keeping my eyes on the housekeeper. "I'm not letting this woman out of my sight."

Molly dashes into the room behind us.

And comes out with her mouth agape and her hands on the sides of her head.

"It's there," Molly says, almost breathless.

I go in there and check for myself.

And it is just as she said.

And so I walk back into the hallway.

"You are indeed Killer Katy Kumquat," I confess.

"Call me Kumquat," she replies solemnly.

"Kumquat," I repeat. "And forgive my initial skepticism. I'm a detective. It comes with the badge."

"I understand," answers Kumquat. "Now let me clean this room before someone hears us talking about superheroes and crime-fighting and obtaining horses. For there are spies everywhere. And you will blow my cover."

"Of course," I answer discreetly. "But I hope you'll see fit to perhaps form an alliance. One in which we give you the benefit of our law-enforcement experience. And you give us a horse."

"Because you can do anything, Killer Katy Kumquat!" declares Molly Moskins. "And we need a horse so we can go *fast*!"

"I know what you mean," says a voice from behind us.

CHAPTER 33

Will You Still Need Me, Will You Still Feed Me, When I'm on the Floor?

"I mean, uh, we really need . . . *to play horsie!*" Molly says, leaping onto my back just as Kumquat disappears silently into the hotel room across the hall.

"Ride, horsie, ride!" Molly adds, kicking me in the sides.

It is a gross indignity, far beneath my noble stature as a detective. But one that I must endure.

For we are suddenly face-to-face with two potential spies.

And they are old.

"Don't mind us," says the man. "We're just a couple of old farts passing through."

"Hush, Peter," says the woman.

"And we're just playing horsie," says Molly from atop my back. "And there's nothing that you should be suspicious of."

I stand, causing Molly to slide unceremoniously to the ground.

"Forgive her," I interject. "The young woman has a tendency to babble incoherently. There's nothing to see here. Please move along."

The old man smiles.

"Well, you look like you're having a lot

more fun than we're having," he says. "We're here for something *un*-fun."

"What is it?" asks a much-too-chatty Molly Moskins.

"Don't listen to him," says the old woman. "We're having lots of fun. We're here for our wedding anniversary."

"Wedding anniversary!" exclaims Molly. "We're in the bridal suite!"

"Well, congratulations to you!" says the old woman.

"*Bridle* suite!" I correct both of them. "As in horse bridles."

THIS AGAIN

"I see," replies the old woman.

"And how long have you two been married?" Molly asks the old couple.

"How long do you think?" replies the old man.

"A hundred years?" guesses Molly.

"Feels like it," he says.

The old woman shakes her head. "He's just joking, sweetie. I'm Vivian, and this is Peter. And it's our sixtieth anniversary."

I glance at Molly and immediately realize that she is about to reveal our names.

To two potential spies.

"Well, hello, Vivian and Peter," she says. "I'm Moll—"

"Molotov Cocktail," I interrupt, shouting the first name I can think of, which just so happens to be a term for a flaming bottle of liquid thrown at tanks.

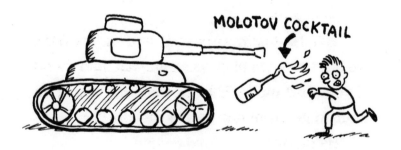

MOLOTOV COCKTAIL

"Interesting," replies Peter. "And what is your name, young man?"

I shout out the first words I see—words that are printed on a bottle hanging out of the old man's sweater.

"Snore Less," I answer.

SNORE LESS

SNORE LESS

The old people stare silently at us.

And smile.

"Well, Molotov Cocktail and Snore Less, we'll let you two play," says the old man. "And if you need us, we'll be in the hall, taking an hour to get from one end to the other."

He pauses.

"So don't get old," he says. *"And stay single,"* he whispers.

I watch as the two of them continue past us. They walk so slowly, you can barely tell they're moving.

The old woman leans her free hand on the man's shoulder. He kisses her on the top of her head.

"Sixty years," she says to him.

"I'd rather have a horse," he replies.

CHAPTER 34
Going Out With a Bing

"Nobody's getting a horse," explains Bing, the hotel's general manager.

← BING

He is visiting us in our suite. And I'm now wishing I hadn't opened the door.

"Listen, I don't know what happened out there on the sidewalk, and I'm hoping you feel a little better now, but you can't stay in the hotel," he says.

"First no horse? Now *this*?" Molly howls.

"Listen, kids. We let you play in the hotel. We gave you all the candy you wanted. But we're not in the baby-sitting business."

"Sorry, Bing," I answer. "But we can't leave."

"And why is that?" he asks.

"The girl's ill in the head," I say, pointing at Molly. "From all the candy you forced on her."

Molly falls over on the couch.

"Oh, great," I add. "Now she's passed out."

"You've passed out?" he asks Molly.

"Yes," answers Molly, staring at him.

"People who've passed out can't talk," he tells her. "And their eyes are usually closed."

"Then I'll be quiet now," she says, shutting her eyes.

Bing stands up and opens the hotel door.

"Okay, kids, you've had your fun. Now get your stuff and let's get going."

I hop off the couch and run to stand between Bing and the hallway.

"Our parents are paying good money for this hotel!" I cry.

Bing looks at me skeptically. "Your parents?" he asks.

"Yep," I answer.

"Yes, well, Emilio said you aren't here with your parents. So try again."

"Emilio?" I answer. "Who's Emilio?"

"The doorman," he says. "Surely you remember him. The young man you terrorized?"

THIS GUY →

"Sir, with all due respect to your hiring practices, Emilio is an incompetent boob. A bumbling idiot. A monkey-brained ninny. And no offense," I add. "As an owner of a business myself, I know how hard it is to get good help. But please, sir, fire the poor slob before he incites further riots."

"Enough," he cuts me off. "I don't have time for this. If my employee says you told him your parents aren't here, I believe his word over that of a little kid. So let's go."

"WE'RE HERE ON A WINDSURFING VACATION WITH OUR PARENTS!" bellows Molly, bolting upright, like a dead person brought back from the grave.

The general manager adjusts his glasses and glares at her.

"I'm feeling fine now, Bing," she adds.

"Little girl," he says, "what are you talking about?"

"Our parents," Molly answers. "They're windsurfing instructors. World champions, in fact. We all go to Lake Michigan and windsurf together. You should see the tricks they can do."

It is a stunning lie. One worthy of a master criminal. And one filled with conviction and details.

All of which I realize she has gleaned from the brochure on the living-room table.

I slide the brochure under a vase.

"And your parents are staying here at the Drakonian?" asks the general manager.

"Bingo, Bing," Molly answers.

"Fine," he says, squinting behind his wire-rimmed glasses. "What room?"

And at that, I see her hesitate. Her mismatched pupils darting back and forth.

So I step in.

Bold. Swift. And defiant.

"OUR WINDSURFING PARENTS ARE RIGHT THERE!" I yell, pointing at the first two people I see in the hallway.

Startling them both.

CHAPTER 35

Meeses Fall to Pieces

No one believed that a ninety-two-year-old man could windsurf with a walker.

So we have been asked to leave the Drakonian.

But not before running into an old friend in the lobby.

"You are the worst fugitive from justice
I have ever seen," I shout at my polar bear.
"How in the world does it help to wear

a *moose head* as a disguise?! Your polar-bear belly is still hanging out! And so is your big rear end!"

Total tries to cover his rear end with his paws.

"And are there even any mooses in Chicago?" I ask.

"Meeses," says Molly.

"Forget it," I tell both of them. "We're leaving."

But the moose-bear stops in the center of the lobby.

"What now?" I ask Total.

He stares at the candy in Molly's hand.

"All right, fine. If you must know, we were given candy by the hotel," I explain to him. "As well as a decent-size suite. Are you happy?"

Total grumbles.

"Yes, there was a large tub," I answer.

Total lies down in the center of the lobby.

"What are you doing *now*?" I ask.

Total begins hitting the floor with his arms and legs.

"A *temper tantrum*?!" I shout. *"Now? Just because you didn't get to use the tub?"*

But Total doesn't listen.

He just keeps flailing at the ground.

And looks like a mutant moose in full cardiac arrest.

"What is it, Timmy?" asks Molly. "What's going on?"

"Somehow we have to get back upstairs."

"But we've been kicked out of the hotel."

"I realize that, Molly," I say between gritted teeth. *"But we have an emergency situation on our hands."*

"Timmy, they'll arrest us!" cries Molly.

"I have a plan," I answer.

CHAPTER 36

Charging Ahead

"We are going to spend a lot of money," I tell Molly Moskins as we walk through the streets of downtown Chicago.

"Oh, how fantastical!" she says. "But how?"

"Your debit card," I tell her. "The one you told me about at the E-Z Daze Motel."

"My debit card?" she answers. "But my parents said it's only for emergencies."

"Molly, we're on a cross-country trek to catch a felon! I think that qualifies as an emergency!"

"I guess you're right," she replies.

We walk past a bookstore that takes up an entire city block.

"Wopell's," says Molly, reading the sign. "Look at this place. It's huge. Let's buy books! Tons of books! Books on fighting crime!"

"We're not buying books, Molly Moskins!

And besides, I know everything there is to know about fighting crime."

"Then we should go to a restaurant and buy the fanciest, most romantic dinner in Chicago!" she replies.

"We're not buying any of those things, Molly Moskins!"

"Then what are we buying?" she asks.

"First we're buying bonbons so that we don't have any more meltdowns from You-Know-Who."

YOU-KNOW-WHO

"Then what?" she asks.

"Then we're buying other stuff."

CHAPTER 37

The Corps of Deceit

"Why'd we have to buy costumes?" asks Molly.

"Because this is how we're getting back into the Drakonian."

"So you're Meriwether Lewis?" she asks.

"Right. The guy with the funny name."

"And I'm the woman who guided them?"

"Correct," I answer. "Sacaga-something."

"But why do we have to be dressed up as

them?" asks Molly. "Why couldn't I just be a kitty cat?"

"Because it would look rather strange for a four-foot-tall cat to stroll into a hotel lobby, Molly."

"But won't this look strange, too?"

"No, it won't look strange! This is where Lewis and Clark came."

"I don't think they came to Chicago, Timmy. I think they went to Oregon."

"But surely they stopped in Chicago."

"Why would they stop in Chicago?" asks Molly.

"Probably for the pizza," I answer.

"I didn't think of that," says Molly.

"You don't think of a lot of things. The point is that people in Chicago are *used* to seeing people like this."

"Really?" she asks.

"Of course," I reply. "We'll fit right in. And when we try to get into the Drakonian, the employees there won't think twice."

CHAPTER 38

It's My Exploring Party and I'll Cry If I Want To

"Oh, God, leave me alone," says Emilio, the doorman.

"I knoweth not what you speaketh of," I answer. "I am Meriwether Lewis."

"Seriously," says the doorman. "I'm gonna have a nervous breakdown."

"We. No. Here. Before," says Molly, trying to sound like the Native Americans she's seen on TV.

"Please go away," says the doorman. "I swear to God. I don't want any trouble."

"Assuredly not, ye fair gentleman," I answer. "We good souls just needeth rest from our long journey acrost this grand continent. Haveth ye any idea how far that is?"

"Is. Far," interjects Sacaga-something.

"Oh, God," says the doorman. "Why are you doing this? If I have one more incident like the last one, I'm done."

"Give. Room. Us," says Molly, turning decidedly stern. "Or. Me. Shoot. Arrow."

Molly pokes him in the side with her finger.

The doorman jumps.

"Sacaga-something!" I shout. "We come in peace! We do not threaten doormen!"

"Well, you didn't say anything about that," Molly answers, her feelings suddenly hurt. "How am I supposed to know if this Sacaga-something was nice or mean?"

"Stay in character," I whisper to Molly. *"Stay in character."*

"No!" says Molly, throwing off her wig. "You've hurt my feelings."

"Oh, God, no," mutters the doorman. "No, no, no, God, no, *please*."

Molly's lower lip starts to tremble.

The doorman fumbles frantically through a large key chain. *"Do not cry. Do not cry. Do not cry,"* he chants.

"Forgive us," I interject, trying to calm the situation. "The gentlelady hath been stressed."

"I don't even HAVE any arrows, Timmy!" shouts Molly, now in full meltdown.

"This isn't happening. This isn't happening," repeats the doorman.

"Surely, the fair lady meant to call me *Meriwether*!" I assure the doorman.

"There!" he cries, yanking a long silver key off the chain. *"Side alley. Blue door. I didn't see you. You never spoke to me."*

I grab Molly by the hand and race for the alley. *"Godspeed, ye fine gentleman,"* I yell back toward the doorman.

Who slumps forward onto his doorman's station. Head down. Eyes tightly shut.

Which is good.

Because he could not have taken what flew by him next.

CHAPTER 39

Pride (in the Name of Detective Work)

We get to our old floor via the back staircase and, once there, have no trouble spotting a hotel room with an open door.

"The housekeeper left it open!" I whisper to Molly. "Just like she did with that room she was cleaning before. See, there's her cart, and now she's in the room across the hall!"

Molly pouts as we peek out of the stairwell entrance down the long hotel hallway.

"But I can't be sure that's Kumquat in there," I add. "It could be one of the Drakonian's other housekeepers. So we can't risk being seen."

"You were mean to me," replies Molly.

"Not now, Molly Moskins. If we hurry, we

can sneak into the open door before the house-keeper closes it again."

"You humiliated me in front of the door-man," she says. "And now I want an apology."

"This is a very delicate moment in the mission, Molly. We just need to get into that room and we'll have our base. Our headquarters. The nerve center for our operation to catch Corrina Corrina, whether she is hiding in this hotel or some other."

I think for a moment.

"We also need a tub for the fat bear."

"I don't care," she responds, much too loudly. "I want an apology."

I think about appealing to her concern for Yergi Plimkin, but I fear another meltdown.

So I swallow hard, aware that a detective must sometimes sacrifice personal pride for the sake of a professional operation.

"Mistakes were made," I whisper to Molly.

"Is that an apology?" she asks.

"It's a detective apology," I answer. "It's all we're allowed to give, by state law."

STATE REGULATION OF DETECTIVES

Section 53(B)(2) — APOLOGIES

**A detective may not say "I'm sorry."
It makes us look bad.**

"Then that's good enough for me!" she says. "I don't want to violate any laws."

"Good for you," I tell her. "That means you've been criminally rehabilitated."

"I know," she answers. "Now let's break into that room!"

CHAPTER 40

Rub-a-Dub-Dub, a Bear and His Tub

We sneak into the open hotel room without incident, and already someone is complaining.

"No, it's not as big as the one we had in the suite," I explain to my polar bear. "But it's the best I can do under these trying circumstances."

Total moans and rolls his eyes.

And the eye roll is the one thing I can't take.

"Why, you ungrateful oaf! We just risked life and limb getting you back into this hotel! All so you can have your stupid little bath and your stupid little bonbons! *And you have the audacity to roll your eyes at me?* That does it! Go sit in the closet! You're getting a polar-bear time-out."

Total stomps into the closet and slams the door.

I look over at Molly. She is using her shoe to pound a thumbtack into the wall.

"And what are *you* doing?" I ask Molly.

"I'm putting up a picture of Yergi," she answers.

"What for?" I ask.

"To inspire us during our investigation. Won't this be our headquarters?"

"Yes, Molly," I answer. "But inspiration's for amateurs. We're professionals. Now, I have to make a phone call. So be quiet."

But there is no quiet.

There is a scream.

CHAPTER
41

He Came in Through the Bathroom Door

It is Kumquat.

And she had been happily listening to her headphones while cleaning the room across the hall.

Until someone went in search of a better tub.

Scared, Total fled back into our hotel room.

And suddenly we have an angry Kumquat on our hands.

"Who told you two you could sneak into this room?" barks Killer Katy.

"We're crime-fighting," I answer. "Like you."

"*I'm* cleaning a hotel room."

"You're *pretending* to clean a hotel room," says Molly Moskins.

"No. I'm really cleaning a hotel room."

"You don't have to keep saying that, Killer

Katy," says Molly. "We won't give away your secret."

"Kids," she says, rubbing her eyes, "you have to go back to your parents, whatever room they're in. You can't stay here."

"We don't need it for very long," I tell Kumquat. "Just long enough to find and arrest Corrina Corrina."

"So Yergi can get his books," adds Molly, pointing to the picture of Yergi on the wall.

"Yes, well, this isn't your room," answers Kumquat.

Molly stands beside the housekeeper. "It is if you say it is, Killer Katy Kumquat. You can do anything."

"Little girl, I am not Killer Katy Kumquat. My name is Talia. I'm just a housekeeper."

"Oh, my," says Molly. "I've heard of this."

"Heard of what?" asks Kumquat.

"Of low points for superheroes. In the movies, they call it the Dark Night of the Soul. It's the point in the film when the superheroes start to doubt themselves."

"But I'm not a superhero!" barks Kumquat.

"I didn't think so, either," I reply, "until I saw you perform the Toilet Seat Wrapper Miracle."

"That was not a miracle!" cries Kumquat, rubbing her forehead.

"It'll be okay, Killer Katy," says Molly. "Remember—Dark Night of the Soul."

"Oh, my goodness," says Kumquat, plopping down upon one of the beds. "I give up."

"There, there," says Molly, patting her on the shoulder. "You are noble and brave."

Kumquat rests her head in her hands.

"Listen," mutters Kumquat, "I'm going to leave now and finish cleaning the room across the hall. So for now, you can keep playing. But when you're done, I need you to go back to your own room and back to your parents. And please, don't make a mess. I don't want to have to reclean this room."

"Thank you, Killer Katy," says Molly.

Kumquat lumbers out of the room.

"Killer Katy," says Molly as Kumquat reaches the door.

"What now?" answers Kumquat.

"Just one more thing."

"What?"

"When you perform your feats of super-hero magic, how do you do it?"

Kumquat sighs. "I wave my magic wand, kid."

Molly gasps. *"I knew you had a magic wand!"* she says. "Can you show us? That is, if it's not a secret or anything."

Kumquat walks out of the room and returns with something in her hand.

"Ta-daaa," she says, waving her magic wand for Molly. "Are you happy now?"

Molly is so astonished, she can barely speak.

But not me.

I am focused.

And as Killer Katy Kumquat departs our headquarters, I know what I must do next.

CHAPTER
42
The Tidy Bowl Girl

"I need more information on Corrina Corrina," I tell Rollo Tookus over the phone.

"Timmy! Where are you?" answers Rollo. "Your mom called my mom! Everyone is *freaking out*!"

"I have no time for hysterics, Rollo. I need more information on Corrina Corrina."

"Oh, my God!" he chants. "Is Molly with you?"

"I cannot get into specifics, Rollo."

"Hi, Rollo!" chirps Molly, who is listening to the call on the bathroom phone.

"Molly! Hang up the phone!" I yell toward the bathroom.

"She *is* with you!" says Rollo. "Oh, my God! Oh, my God! Oh, my God!"

"Okay, you listen to me, Rollo Tookus!" I shout into the phone. "I'm on the verge of solving the biggest case of our generation! But I don't have much time! Now, I need information! Where is Corrina Corrina staying?"

"Oh, my God," he responds. *"Where are you?"*

Before I can answer, Molly begins to respond. "We're at the—"

Her voice abruptly cuts off.

I rush into the bathroom.

And find her stuck in the toilet.

"I was sitting on the toilet and I fell in," she says.

But of course she didn't fall in.

She was pushed.

By an ex-partner who knew enough to save the day.

"I owe you one," I tell the big guy, and grab Molly's bathroom phone.

"Timmy! Timmy! Are you still there?" asks Rollo.

"Yes, I'm still here," I answer.

"But not for long!" says Molly, grabbing the phone back from me.

"Wait!" pleads Rollo.

"What are you doing?" I ask Molly.

"This," she says, hanging up the phone.

"What? Why?" I ask.

"Because," she answers, "I know where Corrina Corrina is."

CHAPTER 43

To Catch a Corrina

Molly's dramatic announcement that she knows the whereabouts of Corrina Corrina is diminished only slightly by the location from which she says it.

"What do you mean you know where she is?" I ask.

"When I fell in the toilet, I just suddenly remembered," she says.

"Remembered what?"

"That before we left for spring break, Corrina Corrina told me about the vacation she was going to take with her dad."

EVIL PERSON

MOLLY

"Did she tell you the name of the hotel?"

"Yeah," she answers. "The Windy Palms. I remember because it sounded so pretty."

I am so happy I could ~~kiss her.~~ ~~hug her.~~ say, "Good job."

But first I must pull her from the toilet.

"Molly, this is the most prestigious moment in the history of detective work."

"It is?" she replies, drenched in toilet water.

"It is," I answer. "You have helped solve the biggest case of my generation."

"Oh, my God," she answers, sounding suddenly like Rollo. "I don't know what to say."

"You don't have to say anything," I tell her. "Just change your clothes. And perhaps freshen up."

"Why?" she asks. "Are we gonna go catch her?"

"We are," I answer. "But first we are going to do something just as important."

"What is that?" she asks, her mismatched pupils wide.

"We're going to celebrate."

CHAPTER 44

Made It, Molly.
Top of the World!

We are thirty storeys above ground at the fanciest, most romantic restaurant in Chicago.

And Molly smells like a grape.

"What's that funny smell?" I ask.

"It's my new lotion. I bought it at the hotel gift shop. It was expensive, but I love it. What do you think?"

"I think you smell like grape jam. If I put peanut butter on your nose, you'd smell like a sandwich."

SANDWICH

"That's the most romantic thing you've ever said to me," she replies, covering her mouth with her hands.

"Don't get carried away, Molly Moskins. This is a professional dinner. A thank-you for your hard work."

"But look at the view," she says. "It's so romantic. We should dance!"

"It's not romantic," I retort. "And we're not dancing! I chose this place because it's symbolic."

"Of what?" she asks.

"Isn't it obvious?"

"No," she answers.

"That tonight I am at the top of the detective world!" I declare.

"Me too?" she asks.

"Well, you were of great assistance," I answer. "And that is being rewarded now."

She smiles.

"Thank you, Timmy Failure. I never get to have dinners like this."

A waiter in a red jacket and black bow tie approaches us.

"Have you two decided on what you'd like for dinner?" he asks.

"Yes," I answer. "I'll have French toast and French fries."

"Oh, how worldly!" says Molly, clapping her hands together.

"And for the young woman?" asks the waiter.

"She'd like the most expensive spaghetti you have," I answer. "And spare no expense. We have a debit card."

I hold up Molly's debit card.

The waiter nods.

"And neither one of us will write on the walls," interjects Molly.

"Very good," says the waiter, walking off.

"You didn't have to tell him that, Molly Moskins. It's assumed at high-end establishments like this."

"Well, I wanted to show him that I was cultured, too," she answers.

Molly glances down at her iced tea, then out toward the Chicago skyline.

I use the opportunity to discuss business.

"I guess I should prepare you for what happens next," I tell her.

"We eat my spaghetti like those two dogs in *Lady and the Tramp*?" She giggles.

"NO, Molly Moskins. I'm being serious."

"Me too," she answers, winking. "Okay, what happens next?"

"Well, as you've probably assumed, tomorrow's arrest of Corrina Corrina will be a major news item. Dozens of reporters. Hundreds of cameras. And I assume you have precious little experience with public relations."

"I don't know," she says. "What is it?"

"Dealing with the press," I answer. "The photographers. Paparazzi can be very pushy."

"Will they all be taking pictures of *me*?" she asks.

"They'll be taking pictures of *me*," I answer. "But you can be in the background."

She thinks about that.

"They'll probably want to take pictures of my pretty eyes," she says, showing off her oddly mismatched pupils. "So maybe I should be at the front."

MOLLY'S VERSION OF PUBLIC RELATIONS

"So what happens after that?" asks Molly.

"After what?" I answer.

"After the case is over. And the cameras go away."

"Well, after that, you're famous."

"So I don't have to go back?"

"Back where?"

"To my family," she adds.

"Well, I don't think it means that," I answer. "I think famous people still have families."

"But they don't have *my* family," she mutters.

I stare at her, silent.

"They don't have my brother," she says. "And they don't have my father."

She pauses.

"And I don't eat like a horse," she adds.

I take a sip of my orange juice.

"So maybe you and I can just keep going," she suggests. "Like to the next city. And the next hotel. And the next investigation. And we never have to look back. You know, because we're famous."

I play with the sugar packets. But say nothing.

"Aren't you gonna talk?" she asks.

I look up at Molly, and then back at the sugar packets.

"Sometimes I don't want to look *forward*," I answer.

She tilts her chin to one side.

"What does that mean?" she asks.

"It means what I said."

"But I don't get it," she says.

"It means I had my own reasons for leaving," I answer. "Okay?"

"You left to catch Corrina Corrina," she offers.

"Well, of course that's why I left," I answer. "But it's more complicated than that."

"You can tell me, Timmy Failure."

"No," I answer. "It's dumb. And I'm a detective."

"So what does that matter?" she asks.

"So we don't have conversations like this."

The waiter refills Molly's glass of iced tea. She waits for him to leave and then leans across the table toward me.

"You don't have to be a detective tonight," she whispers.

I stare out at the tall buildings.

And then back into her mismatched pupils.

And I reach into my pocket.

"Okay. Fine. I wrote it all down," I say.

"What?" she asks.

"What I heard at the E-Z Daze Motel. What Doorman Dave said."

"I don't know what you're talking about," she says.

"Just read it," I tell her. "It'll explain everything."

So I pull my detective log out of my pocket and flip through the pages, looking for the memo I wrote at the E-Z Daze Motel.

THIS ONE →

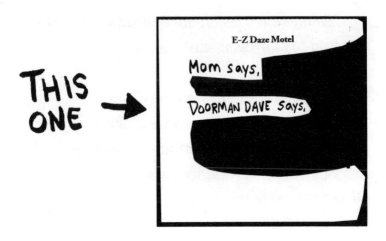

But the memo's not there. And neither is the part I cut out.

"I don't get it," I say. "I had it tucked right here in my detective log. It must have slipped out. Or been stolen. There are thieves *everywhere*."

"Well, tell me anyway," she says.

But as she says it, the waiter approaches with our food.

And Molly stares down at her large plate of spaghetti. And smiles.

And it is the happiest I have ever seen her.

"Tomorrow," I say. "Not tonight. Tonight we're on top of the world!"

I hold out my orange juice. Molly clinks it with her iced tea.

"To first-class spaghetti," she says.

"To the good guys winning," I answer.

CHAPTER
45
They See You When You're Shopping, They Know When You're Awake

"They know every place you've been," says a panic-stricken Rollo Tookus over the phone.

"Rollo," I respond, "I called you from my hotel phone simply because I thought our prior conversation ended abruptly. And I didn't want you to worry. But if you're going to get hysterical again, you're defeating the purpose and we should probably stop talking."

"You shopped at Wild and Wicked Costumes," he interrupts.

Suddenly grabbing my attention.

"Okay, Rollo, what do you know and how do you know it?"

"Your mom told my mom. It's the debit card, Timmy. When you use a debit card, they can track you."

I contemplate that. And how Molly has compromised us with her dreadful debit card.

"They're *tracking* you," repeats Rollo. "Think about it."

So I think about it.

The costume store for the costumes.

The grocery store for the bonbons.

And the restaurant for the dinner.

But they are the only three places we've used it. And we won't use it again.

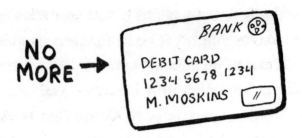

NO MORE →

BANK

DEBIT CARD
1234 5678 1234
M. MOSKINS

"Perhaps it was sabotage," I say aloud. "Perhaps Molly *wants* to get caught."

"That's even worse," Rollo says. "She's your partner. Timmy, you need to go back to your mom."

I pause.

"No," I answer, defiant. "Because it doesn't matter."

"What are you talking about?"

"All they know is that I'm somewhere in Chicago," I respond. "*Allegedly*. But Chicago is a very large town."

I can hear Rollo start to hyperventilate.

"Breathe, Rollo, breathe," I tell him. "You're panicking for nothing."

"Panicking for nothing?" counters Rollo. "Timmy, you're in really big trouble. You need

to go back to your mom! If you go back right now, maybe you won't be in as much trouble!"

"I'm not going back," I answer. "Tomorrow is the culmination of a lengthy—and, may I add, *costly*—investigation. A case that is very high-profile. And a case that *you* gave me. Now if you're jealous of the publicity I shall garner or the fame I will accrue, say it now. Because I won't apologize for it."

"Timmy, stop!" answers Rollo. *"I'm not jealous! I just know they're gonna catch you!"*

I hear a large splash.

"Thank you, Rollo, but I have to go."

"What for?"

"I think someone has fallen into the toilet again."

CHAPTER 46

As Clear as Black and White

But the noise is not from Molly.

It is from Total.

And he is splashing tub water into the air.

"What are you doing *now*?" I ask.

He points toward an empty box of bonbons.

"You're out *already*?" I ask. "We had twelve boxes."

Total drags his large forearm across the surface of the tub water, creating a wave that crashes upon the bathroom floor.

"You're really pushing your luck!" I tell him. "Do you realize that?"

"Realize what?" asks Molly Moskins as she walks into the bathroom, strangely clad.

"And what the heck are *you* wearing?" I ask.

"My zeeba-striped jammies," she answers.

"You look like a convict!" I tell her. "Am I to take this as a subliminal suggestion that you've reverted to your criminal ways?"

"I don't think so," she says. "They're just comfy. Now where am I sleeping?"

I reassess the sleeping situation.

"Well, there are two beds. And I was gonna share one with my polar bear and give you the other."

"Oh, goodie!" she says.

"But I've changed my mind," I answer.

"Why?" she asks.

"Because he doesn't deserve a bed. And you're now a flight risk."

"A flight risk?" she answers. "But I'm a zebra, not a bird," she answers.

"No, Molly Moskins. It means you could *flee*."

"Flee?"

"Yes," I reply. "For your attire has brought back mixed feelings. Of your criminal past. And whether your commitment to a law enforcement future is genuine."

"It is," she says. "Though I may steal the occasional bonbon."

She pops a handful of bonbons into her mouth.

"Oh, good God," I exclaim. "You've stolen again!"

I begin pushing her toward the closet.

"What are you doing?" she asks.

"I'm putting you in the closet, Molly Moskins. I can't take the risk."

"What risk?"

"Of you escaping in the night. Or harming me in my sleep."

"But there's no lock on the closet," she says, poking her head out of the closet door. "I could escape and kiss you on the nose while you're dreaming."

I am suddenly nauseous.

"Molly Moskins, promise you'll do no such thing!" I shout, pushing her large head back into the closet.

"I'm not promising anything," she answers. "Unless I get a pillow," she adds.

I grab a pillow off the bed and throw it into the closet.

"*All* the pillows," she says, now resorting to criminal extortion.

"Curse you, Molly Moskins. It is inhumane to leave a man without pillows."

"Fine," she says, and then makes a puckering sound.

"ARRRRGHH!" I groan, rushing to grab the remaining pillows. "Here!" I say, tossing them one by one into the closet. "You are a menace to society, Molly Moskins."

"But I'm a comfy menace," she answers from behind the closet door.

"It is fortuitous for you that you have done this on my night of triumph, Molly Moskins. Otherwise, my patience would not be as abundant."

But even abundant patience has its limits.

And those limits are suddenly tested.

Not by a zebra-clad criminal.

But by a moose-head-wearing polar bear, who steps out of the bathroom and threatens to make a ruckus in the hotel lobby if he does not get his bonbons.

"More extortion!" I cry.

But he is too big to shove into the closet.

So I leave to buy the bonbons.

CHAPTER
47
Ch-Ch-Ch-Changes

I exit the hotel using the same escape route Molly and I utilized to get to dinner.

Out the back staircase.

Down the stairs.

Into the alley.

And onto the cool, breezy streets.

Where the crisp wind reminds me of the changes to come. For me. For the agency. For my global reputation.

I am tempted to find a phone book right now and look up Corrina Corrina's hotel.

And then walk to that hotel, and find her room, and declare to her that no one can escape the long arm of the law.

But a night arrest would generate very little publicity.

And a detective must always be mindful of publicity.

So I will wait until morning.

But as I check my pockets for the cash to buy Total's bonbons, I find only the debit card.

And that I can no longer use.

I shall have to borrow change from Molly Moskins, I say to myself. *Surely she'll extort all my blankets for this.*

So I turn back.

And walk back down the alley.

And approach the blue door.

And realize I have no key.

This is what I get for rushing out of the room so quickly, I say to myself. *Curse that stupid bear and the felon Molly Moskins! Their selfish, extortionist ways have caused me to forget both the cash and my key!*

So I walk back the length of the alley and around the corner of the hotel. And enter through the revolving front door.

Which is okay.

For it is late.

And there is no doorman.

And there is no receptionist.

And I am safe.

And so I walk across the broad lobby of the Drakonian toward the elevators.

And past the gift shop.

Where I remember a conversation.

The one I had with Molly.

About the lotion.

That she bought here.

And how she most likely paid for it.

With a debit card.

"Timmy Failure," says a police officer, "you're coming with me."

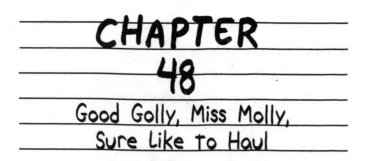

CHAPTER 48

Good Golly, Miss Molly, Sure Like to Haul

I will say one thing for Molly Moskins.

And that is that the girl definitely did not want to get caught.

For when she heard the police coming, she was no longer an in-law, but an outlaw, as she bolted out of the hotel room and into the hallway, seizing a housekeeping cart and swinging it sideways to block her pursuer's approach.

And down the back staircase she went.

Leading police on a chase through much of downtown Chicago.

A chase that went past our fancy restaurant.

And around the costume store.

And into the giant bookstore that Molly was so intrigued by on our walk.

Where Molly ran up and down the aisles, pulling down shelves of used books to block her path.

Through ANTHROPOLOGY and ZOOLOGY.

And BIOLOGY and PHYSIOLOGY.

And ASTROLOGY and TECHNOLOGY.

All without apology.

Until she fell audibly.

In the row marked CRIMINOLOGY.

CHAPTER 49

For Whom the Bells Toll

I am grounded for six months.

No detective agency.

No leaving home.

And per the demand of Molly's parents, no having any contact with her again.

The only exception to all of this is school. It is the one place I can go. And it is the one place I don't want to go.

STILL DON'T LIKE THIS PLACE →

And as bad as it sounds, the punishment was almost much worse.

That is, until I was saved by mitigating circumstances.

"Mitigating circumstances" is detective talk for something that saves your rear end.

And that something was a note given to my mother when everyone was searching for me.

And it said, simply:

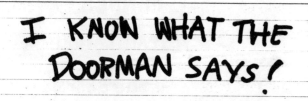

I KNOW WHAT THE DOORMAN SAYS!

And it was signed in that bold and unmistakable handwriting that I had learned to know so well.

For as it turns out, the least articulate human in all of my cross-country adventures had the single most important thing to say.

And had been screaming it all along.

But my mother still did not understand. And neither did anyone else.

So it is then that Molly's little brother produced something I had been looking for since my fancy dinner with Molly in Chicago.

The E-Z Daze memo.

Of which he had not only the part I showed you before:

But the part I cut out as well.

Both of which he took when they fell out of my detective log.

And which, when all taped together, looked like this:

And now you know everything.

CHAPTER 50

All in All, It Was All Just Sand in the Wall

When my mother learned I was in police custody, she and Doorman Dave drove straight there.

And when she met me at the police station, she hugged me for what felt like forever. And then yelled at me for longer.

Weeks have since passed and she has not spoken to me again.

And somehow I like it better when she is yelling.

So when she comes to me on a Saturday morning and says, "Let's take a drive," I know there is more to it than that.

And so we drive for hours in silence until we get to the ocean.

And getting out of the car, she holds my hand as we cross a two-lane highway and climb down the steep bluff to the sand.

And there we sit at the water's edge, staring out at the whitecapped ocean.

Until she finally breaks the silence.

"I just didn't know how to tell you," she says. "And I blew it. I really blew it."

She looks over at me.

"And I will never forgive myself for how you found out. Never. And all I can do now is be as honest with you as possible. Explain everything to you. As I should have done from the start."

I push the wet sand in front of me with my feet, forming a small wall between me and the surf.

"I'm so sorry," she says.

I pack my seawall tightly.

"Timmy, I don't expect you to say a lot, but it would be nice if you could say something."

So I look up from my construction project and say something.

"Everything was fine in that old woman's life until her crazy husband poked a guy with that pitchfork."

My mother stares at me.

"What? What guy?" she asks. "Timmy, what are you talking about?"

I push more sand with my feet, enlarging the seawall.

"It's a painting," I answer. "In Chicago. It's of a couple. I think they're farmers."

THESE TWO →

"Okay," she says. "But what does this have to do with anything?"

I pick up wet sand with my hands and glop it atop the wall.

"The woman in the painting was having a wonderful life," I answer. "Then she decided to get married to some farmer. Probably had a big wedding with lots of hot dogs and everyone was happy."

"Hot dogs?" asks my mother.

"I think he was a pig farmer," I answer.

"I don't know. I'm a detective, not an art critic. The point is that she thought everything was going to be okay. But it wasn't. Because then the old guy bought a pitchfork and, bingo-bango, the whole thing went south."

"Timmy, first off, Dave is not a—"

"Hold on," I continue. "Please. Because then there's the really old guy—"

"*You* hold on," she interrupts. "Who are we talking about now?"

"Different guy. But his name's Peter. I met him at the hotel. He has a walker, he's very old, and he can't windsurf."

"And what does *he* have to do with anything?"

"He was in Chicago with his wife. And they've been married for a hundred years. And he says marriage is bad. So you should probably call him before you make any rash decisions."

"Okay, Timmy, I think I under—"

"And *then* . . ." I cut her off, slowing down for emphasis. "Then there's Molly's dad. You saw that guy for yourself. Did that look fun? Did he look like Mr. Good Times? Mr. Happy Face? Mr. Toodly Doodly?"

"Timmy," my mother says, "I get it."

"Do you?" I ask, slapping more sand onto my seawall.

"I do," she says, reaching out her arms toward me.

"Then do you realize you're ruining every-thing?" I ask.

She grabs me and pulls me into her chest, just as the tide crests over the wall I have built.

"My poor polar bear," I mutter into her shoulder, my voice muffled by her sweater. "How will he get along with Dave? And what about the agency? Dave knows hardly *anything* about it. And what about a detective's strange hours? He knows *nothing* about that."

"Shhhh," my mother says as she rocks me back and forth, the tide wetting my feet.

"And what if he starts liking *maps*?" I add. "Or *pitchforks*? Or starts wearing funny hats? Have you *seen* that thing Mr. Moskins wears?"

AN AFFRONT TO GOOD TASTE

A small wave washes away my seawall, creeping up the sand and around my mother.

"You're sitting in water," I mumble.

"Timmy," she says, gently holding my head in the warm nook between her jaw and shoulder, "I don't know what's going to happen next. None of us do. But whatever it is, whether it's here or in Chicago, you have me. And I have you."

"And we have the bear," I add. "I know he ran up some outrageous hotel bills, but still."

"Yes, the bear, too," she says. "And believe me, we're going to talk about those bills."

"Good luck," I answer. "The polar bear has a very bad attitude."

We stand and walk higher up the beach onto the dry sand.

Where the sound of the surf grows quiet.

"So you're not getting married?" I ask. "And we're not moving to Chicago?"

She kneels, her eyes even with mine.

"I'm still getting married," she answers.

I look down.

"But we're not sure about the move. Not yet, anyway. We have to make sure Dave likes his new job before I uproot both you and me and we move out there to a whole new city."

"That's wise," I answer, glancing up again. "Chicago has men with pitchforks. And giant beans."

"I haven't heard about the beans," she replies. "But it's okay. We have months to decide. It's not like we're going to get married tomorrow. And in that time, Dave can see how he likes his new job."

"He'll hate it," I answer. "The big city is a lonely place filled with buses and guys named Emilio and girls who smell like grapes. Believe me, I know."

She takes my hand and we walk back to the car.

"I know you know," she says as I get into the car. "And if you ever do anything like that again, you'll have a lot more to worry about than girls who smell like grapes."

"It was quite malodorous," I answer as she gets into the driver's seat.

"Timmy," she says, glancing back over the front seat with that cold stare I've been seeing for weeks. "I'm serious."

"I know," I answer.

And as my mother drives, I stare straight ahead.

And see a large bug explode across the windshield of our car.

"Oooh," I say. "Fireworks."

CHAPTER 51

Grapes and Wrath

And there are even more fireworks at the next meeting of YIP YAP.

"Nothing fits in my closet!" screams the peace-loving Toody Tululu to the other board members.

Confusing everyone.

"It's too small! It can't fit my shoes! It can't fit my skirts! It can't fit my hair scrunchies! And what does my mother do? She gets me a dresser! A *small* dresser! And that didn't help at all! I need a new room! I need a new dresser! And I need it now or I'm gonna punch someone in the head!"

"Order! Order!" cries the sergeant-at-arms, Rollo Tookus. "Please, Toody Tululu. No violence! This is a meeting conducted per parliamentary rules."

"Okay, fine," says Toody. "All in favor of punching someone in the head, say 'Aye'!"

"Aye," answers Vice President Nunzio Benedici, idly shoving grapes up his nose.

"Okay, everyone stop right there," declares Rollo. "First, what does any of this have to do with YIP YAP?"

"What does that matter?" replies Toody Tululu. "I have nowhere to put my hair scrunchies."

"Aye," says Nunzio again.

"So today I am officially forming a new charitable organization dedicated to raising money for remodeling my room," announces Toody. "It's called Remodel Everything And Repurchase Entirely New Dresser."

Which, when Toody reveals the sign, forms an unfortunate acronym.

"All in favor of our new charitable group, say 'Aye,'" says Toody.

"Aye," answers Nunzio.

"No, no, no!" cries Rollo. "We are not

forming a new group dedicated to remodeling Toody Tululu's bedroom! We don't even have enough people to vote. Molly's not here."

"Where's Molly?" asks Nunzio.

"She's still grounded, Nunzio," replies Rollo. "She can only go to classes, and that's it."

Nunzio shoves another grape up his nose.

"But more importantly," continues Rollo, "what about YIP YAP? Now that all our money's gone, are we just gonna give up on poor Yergi Plimkin?"

"Oh," says Toody. "About that whole treasury thing."

"What about it?" asks Rollo.

Toody clears her throat before answering.

"I know what happened to the money."

CHAPTER
52
Follow the Bunny Money

"I know what happened to the money!" I shout, gallantly kicking in the door of the YIP YAP meeting.

"Timmy, what are you doing?" asks Rollo. "This is a private meeting."

"Yeah, private," echoes Nunzio.

"Wrong," I tell Nunzio. "This room is on school grounds. Plus your sergeant-at-arms has hired me as a consultant."

Everyone stares at Rollo.

"Well . . ." says Rollo. "I just, uh . . ."

Impervious, I march to the front of the room, my bright-red scarf waving nobly in my wake.

And I climb atop the podium.

"What do you think you're doing?" asks Toody.

"Behold!" I shout to the awestruck crowd. "You are all about to be witnesses to greatness."

Nunzio stops shoving grapes up his nose.

"The Evil One hath robbed you blind!" I shout into a megaphone.

"Who?" asks Nunzio.

"The Evil One," I answer. "A.k.a. the Weevil Bun, the One Whose Name Shall Not Be Uttered, the Beast, the Center of Evil in the Universe, the Thing from the Underworld, Satan, the Worldwide Enemy of Da Goodness In Everything, the Wedgie, the Bad-Eyed Lady of the Lowlands, the Damsel of Darkness, the Mistress of Malevolence."

"Corrina Corrina," adds Rollo.

"Oh," answers Nunzio.

"I have no idea what's going on," says Toody.

"Which is why I am here to explain," I answer valiantly.

"Do you really need the megaphone?" asks Rollo. "There are only four of us in the room."

I put down the megaphone, confident in the power of my voice.

"Well, Rollo Tookus, if you worried less about megaphones and more about who you let in to the meetings of this charitable organization, perhaps things would have turned out differently."

"Huh?" asks Toody.

"Corrina Corrina infiltrated your organization!" I reveal. "And once here in this sacred room, she learned of the vast amount you had stored in your treasury."

"So?" interjects Nunzio.

"So on the eve of her trip to Chicago, she looted said fund."

"She went to *Key Largo*. Not Chicago!" says Rollo. "I told you that already. Your hotel guy wrote it down wrong."

"What's the difference?" I ask.

"About fifteen hundred miles," says Rollo.

"Listen!" I shout. "Brilliance like this is not commonplace."

"Oh, God," says Rollo.

"But then the Weevil Bun panicked," I announce dramatically. "As squirrelly thieves always do. For she knew that if she crossed state lines with that amount of cash, she was sure to get nabbed. So she passed off the loot."

"To who?" asks Nunzio.

"As if you don't know," I answer.

"I don't."

"To *you*!" I declare, staring at Nunzio.

"Me?" asks Nunzio. "Why me?"

"Because, Nunzio Benedici, as Rollo Tookus once told me, *it was you who was molding all the bunnies.*"

"Oh, God," says Rollo again. "Please don't involve me in this."

"Bunnies?" interrupts Toody Tululu. "What bunnies?"

"*Chocolate* bunnies," I explain. "And why was Nunzio molding chocolate bunnies, you ask? Because chocolate bunnies are hollow! The perfect place to hide stolen cash!"

"I'm lactose intolerant," says Nunzio.

"Exactly," I answer, still standing astride

the YIP YAP podium. "So you smashed the poor defenseless bunnies with a hammer and gave all the cash to someone you thought you could trust."

"Who?" asks Nunzio.

My eyes gaze slowly across the room, landing squarely on the rotund kid.

"Me?" shrieks Rollo Tookus. "Oh, my God! He's lost his mind."

"Yes, members of YIP YAP, the man you foolishly elected as your sergeant-at-arms has a long history of criminal activity. Need I remind you who took the Miracle report from Mr. Jenkins's storage cupboard?"

"That was an accident!" cries the rotund kid, rising to his feet.

"Shush your piehole!" I tell Rollo. "Or I'll get out my megaphone again."

"That really hurts my ears," says Nunzio.

"If you think *that* hurts your ears, listen to this next part," I tell the rapt crowd.

"What's the next part?" asks Nunzio.

"That Rollo Tookus panicked! As nervous

ninnies like him always do! And so he smuggled the stolen funds off to the most notorious criminal of our generation."

"Who are we talking about *now*?" asks Toody Tululu.

"MOLLY MOSKINS!" I shout. "A woman whose criminal enterprise is so vast that even the great Timmy Failure has trouble ascertaining its full scope."

(Author's Note: I really don't have trouble with anything, but sometimes I like to act humble.)

"I think I have a headache," says Nunzio.

"I am so confused," adds Toody.

"Well, don't be," I answer boldly. "Because here is where I tell you everything."

"Oh, God," says Rollo. "What now?"

"That Molly Moskins, ever fearless and

cunning, fled the state, bound for Chicago, home of pitchforks and giant beans. And on the way there, she stopped at the E-Z Daze Motel."

I hop off the podium and pace down the center of the table for effect.

"So what happened at the motel?" asks Nunzio.

"There, the villainous Molly Moskins broke under the heat of my relentless interrogation," I answer. "Confessing to the crime and giving me all of the stolen cash."

"So *you* have it?" asks Nunzio.

"No," I answer as I pace the length of the

table like a seasoned prosecutor. "Because I spent it. On miscellaneous travel expenses. I'm a very generous tipper, you know."

"So what does *that* mean?" asks Nunzio.

I suddenly stop pacing and twirl around to face them.

"That I am the criminal," I confess.

"Oh, God," mutters Rollo. "I give up."

"This is ridiculous!" shouts Toody Tululu.

"I'm going home," says Nunzio.

"You listen to me, Timmy Failure," says Toody. "As I was about to explain to everyone before you barged in, there *was* no theft."

"No theft?" asks Rollo.

"*This* I'll stay for," says Nunzio.

"Arrest me," I calmly mutter, placing my hands behind my back. "For the good guy is now bad."

"I was doing the YIP YAP books," continues Toody, "just trying to figure out what we had in the treasury, and I forgot to carry the decimal point."

"You what?" asks Rollo.

"Carry the decimal point. I wrote down

that we had twelve cents. But I goofed. Now, if I had just remembered to move the decimal point three places to the right, you'd see we actually had a hundred and twenty dollars, just like we're supposed to."

Twelve cents → $.12

Then move decimal point three places to the right and TA-DAAAA...

$120.00
(A hundred and twenty dollars)

"So we have the money?" asks Rollo. "It was all just a math error?"

"Yep." Toody smiles. "Sorry for all the hullabaloo."

"We're saved!" cries Nunzio.

I remain standing on the table, my head down, and my hands behind my back.

Toody and Nunzio leave the room. Rollo follows them, but pauses in the doorway.

"I'm going to turn the lights off now, Timmy. You might want to get off the table."

Fearless, I remain motionless, prepared for my arrest.

Rollo turns off the lights and closes the door.

"It's grown dark," I announce.

CHAPTER
53
The King and I

"With my impending arrest, I have no choice but to rehire you," I announce.

The bear is not pleased.

"There's just no other way," I explain. "My imprisonment could be long. I will be separated from friends and associates alike. And I'll need someone to run the detective agency."

But he's too worn-out to argue.

That's because ever since he escaped the Drakonian by riding empty railcars home, he's been working for my mother.

Mostly washing dishes.

All to pay off the exorbitant hotel bills he racked up when he was His Highness in Chicago.

But Total also knows that his rehiring marks the start of a new phase.

Namely, the end of the free bonbons.

Because while there may be a provision in his contract specifying what I have to give him if he's *fired*, there is no such provision for if he's *hired*.

"Remain brave," I tell him, patting him on the back as he dries another dish.

But I know all this grunt work has been hard on him.

So when he is done doing the dishes for

the night, I give him something that I've had with me since Chicago.

And for the first time since coming home, he is happy.

CHAPTER 54

Save the Last

I sneak behind the pockmarked stucco walls of the low-rise building and stoop down beside the trash bins.

Bathed in the cheap neon light of the city, I sit still, the smell of rotten fruit wafting from the soggy pile of cardboard beside me.

For it is a tough life, but it is a detective's life. And it is what I signed up for. And if you want dolled-up glamour, then look somewhere else, kid.

So I wait patiently, immersed in the sound of honking cabs and muscle-car engines. The symphony of the street.

And as the appointed time nears, I glance at my watch. Each tick echoing the beat of this cold detective's heart.

Aware of the risk. But staring right down the barrel of it.

And when the click of heels across broken pavement grows near, I know that danger has arrived.

In a little pink dress.

"Hello, Timmy Failure!" chirps Molly Moskins.

"Not so loud, Molly!" I answer. "I'm not supposed to be here!"

"Me either!" she says. "I'm grounded just like you!"

"The world's gone mad," I remind her.

"I know!" she replies.

We are in the back parking lot of the E-Z Daze Motel.

Well, not *the* E-Z Daze Motel.

That one was too far away.

But it's a chain. And this one is not far from home.

"Did you hear that Yergi Plimkin got his books?" asks Molly.

"I did not," I answer.

"Yes, a lot of them. But they weren't in his language. So he uses them to mount his llama."

"I'm glad," I tell Molly Moskins, "but I didn't ask you here so we could talk about llamas."

"Why *did* you ask me here?" asks Molly.

I don't answer, but I know why.

And that is because detectives are tough men, but decent men.

And so, after making sure no one is around, I press PLAY on my portable music player.

And to the tune of flamenco guitar, I make somebody's night.

All while the E-Z Daze man smiles down on me.

Forgiving me as he should.

The bad guy now good.

STEPHAN PASTIS is the creator of the *New York Times* bestselling Timmy Failure series, the first of which was a 2014 BookTrust Best Book Awards winner, a runner-up in the 2014 Sainsbury's Children's Book Awards and listed as one of 100 Children's Modern Classics by *The Sunday Times*. He is also the creator of *Pearls Before Swine*, an acclaimed comic strip that appears in more than seven hundred newspapers and boasts a devoted following. Stephan lives in northern California, USA.

Read on for a sneak peek
at the next book in the
Timmy Failure series

Author's Note:
From the Desk of
Timmy Failure

This book was not meant for publication. It is a private record of a sensitive time in my life as a detective.

And then the manuscript was stolen. Which is how it ended up in your hands.

So please put the book down and stop reading.

I don't know much about you.

But I do know this:

You don't have a lot of respect for an Author's Note.

Because when the Author's Note on the previous page asked you to put this book down and stop reading, you took that to mean:

HEY! KEEP READING!

So let me get right to the point.

I am Timmy Failure. I am a detective.

And I am banned from detective work.

BANNED

You don't need to know the details.

You just need to know that none of the detective work you are about to read about was supposed to happen.

And the only reason I kept a record of it at all was that I knew I was going through the most productive career phase ever experienced by a detective.

So if you're going to keep reading (and so far, I haven't been able to stop you), I need you to raise your right hand and swear the following oath:

I, (state your name), do hereby agree to never reveal the contents of this book to anyone, including, but not limited to, Timmy's mother, who would crush Timmy like a bug if she ever found out he was doing detective work during the time of his banishment.

And I do hereby further agree that if any part of this oath shall be broken by me, intentionally or otherwise, I shall be subjected to the following punishment:

I will be covered in mustard and eaten by a polar bear.

CHAPTER
1

Not Really the Start of the Story, but Intriguing Nonetheless

I am Hawaii Joe.

And my sunglasses are large.

As is my polar bear.

Whom I have named after the state fish of Hawaii:

Humuhumunukunukuapuaa.

"Come here, Humuhumunukunukuapuaa," I say to my polar bear. "Because I am about to make an announcement to all of the employees of our detective agency."

(Well, it is not really *our* detective agency. It is *my* detective agency. But I like to be inclusive so as not to offend the feelings of Humuhumunukunukuapuaa.)

So I press the red intercom button on my telephone.

"Greetings, employees of Failure, Inc. This is your founder, president, and CEO, joined by my administrative assistant, Humuhumunukunukuapuaa."

As I talk, I see my employees begin to gather outside the glass wall of my office.

"It is hard to imagine, but it was not long ago that I, Timmy Failure, was doubted by the petty masses, including my rotund best friend, Rollo Tookus; my tangerine-scented classmate, Molly Moskins; and my lifelong foe, She Whose Name Shall Not Be Uttered But Can Now Be Uttered Because We Have Defeated Her and No Longer Care, Corrina Corrina."

There is a roar of approval from the employees.

"But those days are a distant memory. And now look at us. We are a massive detective agency with over a hundred employees, multiple offices, a global reach, and free donuts every Friday."

Everyone applauds.

"Speaking of the donuts, I understand there has been a battle going on for the maple bar ones."

Humuhumunukunukuapuaa nods.

"My administrative assistant here informs me that some of you have been seen racing to the donut box and licking the maple bar donuts so as to claim them as your own."

A few of the employees look away.

"I am speaking specifically of Liz Bicknell, Carter Hasegawa, and Ann Stott. Please stop licking the maple bar donuts."

Heads down, Liz, Carter, and Ann leave the group of gathered employees in shame.

"Now some of you are probably wondering how we got here. How I took my grand vision of a detective empire and made it reality."

Humuhumunukunukuapuaa coughs.

"How *we* made it reality," I say, correcting myself.

Humuhumunukunukuapuaa smiles.

"We did it by following one guiding moral principle. A principle that I have had printed upon a banner that will now hang in our office forevermore. And it is this:"

You'll have to read *Timmy Failure: The Book You're Not Supposed to Have* to find out what happens next...